Surrender to Peace

by

Rose Allen McCauley

Table of Contents

Dedication

THIS book is dedicated to all those whom God has blessed with some form of the autism spectrum, either personally or by a family member.

I have been blessed to have Austin Allen as my nephew for twenty-one years now, and have loved watching him mature into a very friendly young college man who will go as far as God leads him if he will always listen to and obey Him.

My husband and I have also been blessed by meeting the Bridgeman family and their special son, Scott, for whom God also has a special Kingdom plan.

This story is also dedicated to my sister Becky Villier and her husband Captain Stevie who really is a boat captain in New Orleans. May God bless them and give them a lovely place like Puerto Rico for retirement, only closer so we can visit more often.

"The Lord your God is with you,
He is mighty to save.
He will take great delight in you,
He will quiet you with His love,
He will rejoice over you with singing."

Zephaniah 3:17

CHAPTER 1

Chapter 1

JOY Worth stared out the commercial jet's small window at the beauty of the island awaiting her. The canopy of brilliant blue sky and blazing sun couldn't touch the chill enveloping her broken heart. The tropical heat of San Juan, Puerto Rico was a far cry from the frigid weather she'd left in Chicago this morning. And far from the frozen temperatures of her heart. How could she have been so clueless?

The ding signaling the seat belt sign startled her. The passengers around her rose from their seats, moved into the narrow aisle, and reached for their overhead luggage. Like a robot, she followed their lead, even though she wasn't looking forward to her "honeymoon-for-one."

Perspiration formed across her forehead as she carried her small bag down the metal steps to the tarmac. She strode into the terminal, then shrugged off her jacket. Cool air skimmed over her bare arms, drying her wet skin.

Joy followed the signs to baggage claim. Her suitcase snaked along the steel conveyer belt. Alone. *Just like I am.*

She found a cab waiting at the curb, then slid in and

smiled at the driver. "The Inn of the Dove Bed and Breakfast, *por favor*."

The driver nodded and merged into traffic.

Joy looked from side to side, soaking up the ambience of her temporary home for the next two weeks. Anything to get her mind off the betrayal.

A glimpse of ocean through the window momentarily lifted her spirits. The B and B's web page showed their location in the old part of town close enough to walk to many sites, yet only a few steps from the beach. Could they be getting close?

The cab stopped right at the edge of Old San Juan. Glancing to the right, she saw the Inn of the Dove sign on a lovely tile-roofed building. Peace and tranquility surrounded her. A black wrought iron fence enclosed the inn, a stark contrast against its welcoming yellow outer-walls. The yard and porch area overflowed with lush greenery—plants, bushes, even tall trees. She'd love to paint this scene.

Departing the cab, she drew in a breath of roses and another familiar scent. Honeysuckle? She looked around, but saw no honeysuckle, just a red plant with small flowers.

Turning, she paid the driver and grabbed her bag. "*Gracias.*"

"De nada, Señorita."

As she walked through the gate, she drew in a deep breath of the flower-perfumed air. The view from this side of the fence brought even more pleasure than the outside. A fountain gurgled in one corner of the yard. She loved this place already. The online pictures hadn't done it justice.

She picked up her bags and entered at the door marked

Lobby. Her heels clicked against the terra cotta tiles. Colorful upholstered furniture and a vase of white orchids on a table welcomed her.

A regal woman in a flowing yellow dress stepped out from behind the reception desk and walked toward her. "Welcome, *Señorita*. Do you have a reservation?"

"Yes, my name is Joy Worth and—"

"Ah, *Señorita* Worth, I am Ramona Sanchez." The woman gave her a welcoming hug like a longtime friend. Joy considered her a friend, although they'd never met in person. They had spoken countless times about clients for the travel agency where she worked. Her familiar, motherly voice had encouraged Joy to pour out her woes to this woman the night Ricky told her they were through. He wasn't marrying her. He didn't love her. He loved someone else.

The woman pulled back and searched Joy's eyes. "We have spoken on the phone many times to make arrangements for others, and now you are finally here, *sí*?"

"*Sí*. You were so kind and generous to change my reservation to a smaller room. *Gracias*."

"*De nada*." *Señora* Sanchez cupped her hand and beckoned Joy to follow her down a corridor. "Come, let me show you your room. You can freshen up, then take care of the details later."

How wonderful. This kind lady must be reading her mind. Joy couldn't wait to get out of the clothes she'd worn all day.

Señora Sanchez opened a door wide and motioned Joy in. "It is small, but comfortable, and you have a door to our back porch. You can go and come through your patio when you wish to walk to the beach."

Joy studied the room, then smiled, something she hadn't done in days. Ever since…no, she wouldn't go there.

Pristine white sheets and duvet covered the bed, adorned with colorful pillows. A riot of pink and purple flowers outside her window brightened the room. Next to the bathroom sat a dresser and television. Sliding glass doors led to the porch filled with flowers and greenery similar to the front entry. "Lovely. I can't thank you enough."

Señora Sanchez nodded. "I am glad you're pleased. Let me know of anything you need. We want our guests to be happy." She handed Joy her room key then left.

Happy? Not an emotion Joy had experienced since the breakup. Sitting on the bed to remove her heels, she fell back, travel weary, her heart aching. She stared at the white ceiling. This should have been her honeymoon. With her groom. Not alone.

AN hour later, after a short pity party, then a nice long shower, Joy dressed in pink Capris with a crisp white sleeveless blouse and white sandals. She glanced in the mirror. Her green eyes which her friends told her were her best feature stared back at her, rimmed in red, so she put on her sunglasses.

Señora Sanchez stood at the counter checking in an elderly couple. She handed the man two keys. "Just in case you want to go somewhere separately."

The man put an arm around his wife. "I ain't letting this pretty lady out of my sight. No, sir. Someone else might make a play for Ida."

His wife blushed. "Harry, don't you worry. I'm not going anywhere we don't go together."

Joy smiled at the couple on the outside, but inside she groaned. Together. If only her fiancé had looked at her like that. Thinking back, she realized he never had. If only she'd noticed the signs before the wedding invitations were sent, and all the plans made and paid for—with her money.

As the couple walked down the hall, *Señora* Sanchez came out from around the counter. "Please sit with me a few minutes. It will be so nice to talk in person after our years of chatting on the phone. I made some *limonada*, or do you prefer a soft drink?"

"Lemonade sounds refreshing, *gracias*."

Señora Sanchez returned with two tall glasses, then went back to a room off the lobby and carried out a plate of cookies and breads.

Joy took a sip, then another one. The cool liquid quenched her thirst.

"I am so happy to meet you in person, *mi amiga*. Please, call me Ramona."

"If you will call me Joy." She twirled a piece of her long hair around a finger. "And I do appreciate your listening to my outburst the night Ricky broke our engagement. With my mother dead, and my father so withdrawn, I needed to tell someone."

"I understand. Some things are better understood by another woman." Ramona patted her hand. "I am always here if you need a listening ear. Now, what do you have planned for this evening?"

"I want to take a stroll down the main street and find someplace to eat a light supper. Do you have any suggestions for authentic Puerto Rican food that isn't too spicy?"

"A friend from church runs *Maurita's Restaurante* where you can get the best *Mofongo* around."

"Mo-what?"

Ramona laughed. "It's a dish of mashed plantains filled with whatever you like—meat, or seafood, and vegetables. Tell Maurita you want something light and not spicy. Maybe some chicken with rice and corn. She'll point you in the right direction."

Joy's stomach growled at the mention of food. "Thanks. And for dessert?"

"Come here and eat some sweetbreads. Or you can always stop for an ice cream or shaved ice on your way back. No worry about the calories. You will walk it off on your day tour tomorrow of the *El Yunque* rain forest. My son Marcos will drive you and some other guests there in our van."

Joy wanted to protest, but hunger and exhaustion stopped her. She stood. "Can you give me directions to the restaurant?"

Ramona rose and walked with her to the front gate. She nodded to the left. "Go this way for one block, and the *restaurante* will be on the corner after you cross the street. Tell Maurita I said *hola* and will see her at church tomorrow morning."

"*Sí. Gracias.*" Joy stepped out onto the busy sidewalk, then moseyed along, taking in the sights and aromas. Soon, she reached the corner and read the sign for the eatery across the street.

The door to the restaurant stood propped open. As she entered, soft music with a Caribbean beat and a short woman with dark, curly hair welcomed her. "Table for one?"

"*Sí.*"

The lady led her to a table by an open window, then handed her a menu. The top of the menu next to the restaurant's name showed a picture of the woman before her.

Joy raised her head. "Are you the owner?"

"*Sí.*"

"I am staying at the Inn of the Dove. Ramona Sanchez told me to tell the owner she will see you at church in the morning, and to ask for a non-spicy *Mofongo* with chicken."

The owner's face lit up in a bright smile. "Please tell Ramona I will be there. And I will make sure the chef puts no spices in your *Mofongo*, but I will bring a small dish of several spices you may sprinkle on yourself."

"That sounds wonderful. And a soft drink, *por favor.*"

"What kind? We have *la cola*, or our special Puerto Rican drink is *Coco Rico*. A fizzy soda with a coconut flavor."

"I'll try the Coco Rico, *gracias.*"

After the owner left, Joy stared out the window, her eyelids almost closing in spite of the bounty of multicolored flora only inches away. She'd been out of bed by four thirty to catch her early flight. Jet lag overtook her.

Maurita returned with her drink, and some chips and salsa. "The salsa is mild. Hope you enjoy it."

"Muchas gracias."

"De nada."

The chips and salsa refreshed her, but she wanted to save room for the—what was it called? She searched her brain… *Mofongo*. She hoped it tasted better than its funny name.

She ate a little more then pushed the remainder of the chips away.

Maurita raised an eyebrow as she set down a huge plate of food shaped into a tall beehive-like mound. Joy had never seen anything like it. "You no like the chips and salsa?"

"I liked them too much, but I was afraid I wouldn't be able to eat my meal if I ate anymore."

The owner grinned, then set down a smaller plate with compartments and several tiny spoons. "I hope you like the *Mofongo* as well. Here are the spices to try. We must put some meat on your bones while you are here."

Joy had dieted for the past four months, trying to look good in her size six wedding dress. Heartache had stolen her appetite after the breakup, so she now weighed less than she had in high school.

After the first bite of *Mofongo*, her resolve surrendered to the delicious flavors of the exotic dish. She didn't want to stop, but had to when her stomach protested. She sipped on her *Coco Rico*. Ahhh.

Maurita stopped by her table and gave a knowing grin. "I see you liked your *Mofongo*, but…"

Joy cradled her stomach with her arms. "It was delicious, but I am too full. I tasted the garlic in the *Mofongo*, but what are all these spices, *por favor*?" She pointed to the plate with the spoons.

"Cilantro, coriander, and oregano. Which one did you like best?"

"Coriander, I think. New to me, but went well with the *Mofongo*."

"I agree." She slipped a bill onto the table. "I hope you will visit us again. You may pay at the front cash register."

"*Muchas gracias*. I couldn't have asked for a better first meal in Puerto Rico."

The owner's eyes twinkled with pleasure. "If you are happy, I am happy."

After she paid her bill, Joy crossed over to the opposite side of the street to window shop some different stores on her return trip. The sky lit up with pinks and oranges and purples, so it must be close to sunset. Maybe tomorrow she could see the sunset on the beach, but she didn't want to chance getting lost in the dark until she knew her way around.

She passed up the ice cream and shaved ice stands, too full and tired to stop. She would tell Ramona she was too exhausted to go on the tour in the morning.

When she entered the lobby, a man who had to be Ramona's son stood behind the desk.

He smiled. "You must be *señorita* Worth. I am Marcos Sanchez. My mother said you were wearing pink and white, and to tell you she called and added you to the tour tomorrow. No charge because you have sent us so much business in the past."

Drat. It would be rude to turn down their gift. "*Gracias*. What time do I need to be ready?"

"Breakfast is from seven until nine, and we plan to leave at nine. Be sure to wear hiking shoes."

"*Muchas gracias*." She'd go check out the kitchen first. Perhaps she could find a sliver of Ramona's sweetbread she could stow in her room for breakfast so she could sleep an hour later.

She might even eat a small piece tonight. I need some sweet dreams. What will tomorrow bring?

Chapter 2

JOY slept so hard, she couldn't recall any dreams when her cell alarm went off at eight. She stretched, energized by the long restorative sleep, then ate the banana bread from the night before. While drinking a bottle of water, she dressed as Marcos had suggested—a thin long-sleeved shirt, khakis and hiking boots with socks. Not the most glamorous outfit she owned, but it served its purpose.

She put her hair in a ponytail, added a ball cap, then pulled the tail through the slit in the back. No makeup except some sunscreen. No need to dress up. She didn't know anyone here and didn't want to meet anyone either. Her dream of marrying and having a family before turning thirty had dissolved into a puff of smoke. She would concentrate on her career instead.

Drawn by the aroma of freshly-brewed coffee wafting down the hall, Joy joined the others in the kitchen, then poured a cup of the steaming java. Stronger than her usual, but the taste grew on her.

Marcos Sanchez appeared and nodded at the group. "*Buenas dias*. The van is out front, so you may start loading now. We'll leave in five minutes."

Joy double-checked her backpack to make sure her sunscreen, sunglasses, several bottles of water, and camera were inside before walking to the van. The elderly couple from last night went in front of her, hand in hand.

Harry held the inn door for Ida, then motioned for Joy to precede him. "Good morning, Miss. We're the Judds from Mississippi. Is this your first trip to Puerto Rico?"

"Yes. I'm Joy from Chicago. Have you been here before?"

Ida smiled. "Yep, this is our seventh time. We've been coming once a year since we spent our honeymoon here."

Tears stung Joy's eyes at the word honeymoon. "So you came here on your honeymoon seven years ago? How romantic."

Harry joined them. "It is a romantic place. Have you got a fella back home, Joy?"

Her face heated. "No, uh…"

Ida gave him the evil eye. "Gentlemen don't ask questions like that, Harry. Of course a pretty young thing like her has a fella somewhere."

Marcos slid open the van door.

Joy hoped he hadn't overheard their conversation. She scrambled into the back corner of the van and positioned her backpack against the window to lean against. Let them think she'd fallen asleep.

In a couple minutes the motor vroomed to life, and the van moved down the street.

Next thing she knew, the van stopped with a jerk. She

opened her eyes to see the others climbing out. Had she slept another hour?

As she paused at the door, a taller version of Marcos held out his hand to assist her. His brother?

Marcos gathered them all in a circle. "As I mentioned on the drive over, my cousin, Forest Ranger Benigno Cook," he motioned to the taller man, "will be your guide today. You pronounce his name Beh-neeg-no. He is an expert on our Puerto Rican horticulture and the *El Yunque* rain forest, so be sure to grill him about anything you want to know. I will pick you up at the Big Tree Trail Head at four PM to drive you home in time for your evening meal on the town. Benigno will provide a picnic lunch on your hike." He waved as he slid into the van seat. "*Hasta la vista.*"

The tall cousin—what was his name?—led them over to a map of the trail. "I'm glad you all dressed for hiking because we will be covering two of *El Yunque*'s many trails today. As you can see, our rain forest covers over twenty-eight thousand acres, so we will not see all of it on a day trip. Some people come back time after time to hike them all."

Harry put an arm around his wife's shoulders. "We've done six of the trails so far, right, honeybun?"

"Right, Harry." Ida grinned up at him.

The Ranger pointed to the map. "This is the parking lot where we are now, and this is the trail we will be taking this morning, *La Mina* Trail." He dragged his finger over a green line then stopped at an icon of water. "We will hike for about an hour to the *La Mina* Falls, where any of you who wish may swim in the natural pool at the base of the falls. Then we will enjoy our picnic before hiking out the Big

Tree Trail." His finger moved across the map to another icon. "This is where we will meet Marcos by 4 PM. Any questions?"

Ida raised her hand. "Can we stop along the way to rest or take pictures?"

Their guide nodded. "Each trail takes less than an hour to hike, so we have plenty of time to enjoy the scenery and take pictures. Life is a journey, not a race, no?"

Startled, Joy raised her head. He'd quoted one of her favorite sayings. The man smiled straight at her.

BENIGNO normally led a group without favoring any one traveler. But the loneliness in her green eyes tugged at his heartstrings.

She'd turned her head, so he couldn't tell if she'd noticed. *Cool it, Cook. Keep everything professional.*

"Any more questions before we start?" His gaze circled the group before returning to her. "I do ask you to keep me or someone else from our group in sight at all times. The park can get pretty crowded, and we don't want to lose anyone before lunch."

A few in the group chuckled.

"All right, let's be on our way." He turned and led them down the trail single file until he stopped beside a tree about ten feet tall with red flowers. "Please ask for information about any flora or fauna you see. I wanted to first point out the Puerto Rican hibiscus, our state flower. Since this tree is already blooming, it is at least five years old."

He continued down the trail. Keep your mind on your job, not on the beauty with the dark hair with copper highlights and gorgeous green eyes.

JOY stopped to take a couple photos, then hurried to catch up.

The group had paused for another plant lesson. Ida wanted to know the name of a purple bush.

"This is one of our bougainvillea varieties. Notice the papery thin flowers." The Ranger held the delicate flower in his sturdy hand.

This plant looks like the one on Ramona's front porch. "Can they also be red?"

"Yes, and pink, or white, or sometimes a combination of two colors. Are you familiar with them?"

"I noticed some red ones on Ramona's front porch last night. Their scent reminded me of honeysuckle back home."

He smiled at her again. "You are very observant. Some varieties of bougainvillea do smell like honeysuckle, but most have no scent at all."

Joy raised her camera and took a couple more shots of the blossoms.

They strolled for the next hour, punctuating their journey with pauses to question their guide or to capture images of the lush, tropical vegetation..

The sound of rushing water reminded her of the waterfall

he'd promised. She hadn't worn a swimsuit, but hoped to take off her shoes and socks and wade in the water to cool off.

She rounded a bend, the sight of the water cascading down the hillside stalling her steps. The raw power and beauty swept away her self-pity for an instant.

Their guide turned to face the group, then extended his hand toward the Falls. "*Cascada La Mina.*" The awe on his face reflected her own.

Cascada La Mina. She thrilled at the sound of the words rolling from his lips in a melodious baritone.

"I hope you all brought some kind of beach shoes to protect your feet from sharp rocks and the chilly water. We'll stay here an hour if the group likes. If you're not getting in, feel free to roam around the area and take pictures as long as you keep me in sight. I'll be right here." He climbed onto a large rock ledge.

The description of sharp rocks and chilly water encouraged Joy to enjoy the view from land, so she walked around and snapped several pictures of the Falls. She spied a bridge up the trail a short distance away that made a perfect vantage spot for more pictures.

She circled around a tropical bush and approached the ranger. "Mr. Cook, I wondered if I could go up to the bridge." She pointed in the direction. "To get some shots from a different angle."

A friendly smile covered his face. "Please, call me Benigno, or Ben if that's easier. And what is your name, Miss…?"

"Worth, but you may call me Joy."

"What a lovely name. Just like the view from the bridge!" Warmth rushed to her cheeks at his compliment. "I'd prefer you wait until we cross that bridge when we start up the new trail. We'll stop there so you and the others can take some pictures there."

"Thanks. I'll look for more close-ups of the flora."

"But don't forget the fauna. Puerto Rico has over two hundred species of birds as well as hundreds of reptiles and amphibians. You'll find them all over the forest floor."

Her pulse jumped at that statement. "I'll keep my eyes open for them, too." She paused. "When you said reptiles, did you mean poisonous snakes?" She sucked in a breath.

"There are poisonous snakes in Puerto Rico, but not in *El Yunque* rain forest, so no worries."

The breath she'd been holding whooshed out of her lungs in relief. "That's good to know."

He grinned, a deep dimple forming in his bronzed cheek.

"Ranger Cook," another traveler interrupted.

Joy turned, taking care where she stepped so she wouldn't disturb any wildlife. Several green lizards skittered away as she walked down the trail. She also heard a noise like "ko-ke" but wasn't sure if it were a bird or something else. She raised her eyes to the cloudless blue sky filtering through the canopy of the taller trees, but didn't glimpse any birds as she moved on.

Not able to see Ben or anyone from the group, she re-traced her steps and returned to the falls. Sitting on a rock, she closed her eyes and allowed the flowing water to calm her spirit. After a few minutes someone tapped her on the shoulder. She stared into the ranger's blue eyes. *Blue*?

With understanding in his eyes, he apologized, "You looked so peaceful, I didn't want to disturb you, but we're leaving for the picnic grounds now. We'll stop on the bridge for photos on the way. Are you ready?"

She nodded, unable to speak, mesmerized by his startling blue eyes.

He offered her his hand, and without hesitation, Joy placed her palm against his, surprised by her reaction. Were the heat and humidity affecting her?

Flushed, she stood, pulling her hand away. "Thank you." She turned quickly to pick up her bag, then meet up with the others.

Everyone loved the view from the bridge, and took several photos. Someone suggested a group shot with the Falls in the background, so Ben offered to snap the scene on several cameras.

They reached the picnic area in fewer than twenty minutes. Ben set his backpack on one of the tables. Chatting to the people gathering around, he emptied his pack. Was it bottomless? She couldn't believe the growing selection of food on the table—cheese and crackers, apples, protein bars, and juice boxes.

He also fastened a plastic bag to the end of the table with a clip. "Our motto in *El Yunque* is 'Pack it in, pack it out,' so put all trash in this bag, *por favor*.

He glanced her way and smiled. She returned a smile of her own. Was the intense beauty surrounding them working magic on her mood? For the first time since she'd arrived, she was glad she'd come.

AS they continued after lunch, Benigno stopped more often for those who needed to rest on the steeper trail.

During a break, he stepped beside Joy and spoke quietly, "There is a rare canario flower a few feet away." His gaze darted to the yellow blossom. "Come, it will only take a second."

Joy picked up her camera. "Great."

After only a trio of steps, he froze and pointed. A coqui hopped onto the flower. What a shot if they could take it without making any noise. Lifting a finger to his lips, his voice barely whispered. "Do you want a close up?"

Joy nodded, her green eyes larger than the canario bloom. Raising her camera, she followed his lead.

He bent to hold a tree limb out of her way.

She leaned over so close, he caught a whiff of her perfume.

Wisps of her silky soft hair, caught by the breeze, trailed across his arm. He tried to convince himself he would have done this for anyone in the group, but it wasn't true. He'd lost count of the times he'd caught himself following her progress, watching for her smile.

When she poised her camera over the flower, a wide pale band of skin circled the base of her ring finger. The void explained the sadness that filled her eyes, but what did it mean?

Why did he care? Like so many who came before her,

she was a tourist who would be gone in a few days—the first tourist, however, he would miss.

Chapter 3

JOY berated herself all the way home. Why had she paid Ben a bit of attention? Why did she court trouble by getting close to a guy? Hadn't she learned her lesson?

When they arrived at the inn, she went straight from the van to her room. Ramona waved at her and smiled, but Joy continued on without a word. All of the surprises from the past week were catching up with her. Comfort was the only thing she longed for, so put on her pajamas and lay on the bed.

Her heart ached. This non-honeymoon had gone from bad to worse.

How could she be attracted to a guy she'd only met a few hours ago? How could she ever trust her fickle heart again?

She'd never understood men.

Her dad wasn't interested in what he called her "girly things"—like music, dance, art, and scrapbooking. When her mother died soon after Joy's tenth birthday, Joy had tried to get him to share those things with her as her mom had done, but he was too much of a loner. He liked reading, fishing, playing games on the computer, watching television, things he could do by himself. She had tried to join him on a fishing trip—once. He said she talked too much and scared the fish away. Why couldn't he see it was the only time she'd ever had him all to herself?

When he'd given her the elaborate camera the week before the planned wedding, it had been a symbol to her of his attempt to understand her in some small way. A much fancier camera than she needed, but she took it as proof of his confidence in her, so she would learn to use it and make him proud.

Knocking sounded at her door. When she opened it, Ramona stood framed in the light of the hallway. "Is something wrong? My shift is over, but I wanted to make sure you were all right before I left for the evening."

Joy intended to tell her she was fine, just tired. Instead, at the genuine concern she read in Ramona's eyes, she stepped toward the older woman who encircled Joy in her arms.

Ramona rubbed her back like her mother used to do. "There, there, it'll be all right. Do you want to talk about what's bothering you?"

They sat down on the bed, side by side.

Joy reached for a tissue from the bedside table. "It's not any one thing. It's everything. All the mistakes I made by accepting Ricky's proposal, then making all the honeymoon plans alone, even paying for it myself. I should have seen his lack of commitment. But I've never understood my dad or any man."

"Many women say the same thing, *mi amiga*. And many men think we don't understand them. Like the saying, "Men are from Mars, women are from Venus."

Joy chuckled. "I've heard that, but other people seem to find someone who understands them. Why can't I?"

Ramona stared into her eyes. "You lost your closest friend, your mother, when you were ten. Did you have no other women to talk to?"

"Not often. My dad's parents were both dead, and he didn't encourage me to visit my mom's family much. He would drop me off on Christmas morning at their house, then pick me up that evening. Same thing on my birthdays."

"How about ladies at your church?"

"My mom used to take me to church where I accepted Christ at the age of nine, but my dad never went. After Mom died, one of her friends picked me up each Sunday. But a few months later, Dad told me he didn't want to have to get up early on Sunday morning, so for me to tell her this would be my last time. I did read my Children's Bible every day, and later found my mom's Bible in a closet. I devoured it and her notes. One of the first things I did after I got my driver's license was start going to church every Sunday."

"I'm glad to hear that. I'll add my prayers to yours for your dad's salvation."

"Thanks, he's so different from most people, it's hard to talk with him.

"That's sad, but God calls all of us into a relationship with Him, different or not. Would you like to go with me to church in the morning?"

"Yes, if I can pull myself out of this jet lag to crawl out of bed."

"Good. Do you plan to go out for dinner tonight, or can I

bring you some tea and toast since you're already in your pajamas?

Joy glanced down at her attire, sniffled, then smiled. "You're spoiling me, Ramona."

"Everyone needs to be spoiled sometime. I'll be right back."

True to her word, Ramona tapped on the door a few minutes later. She carried a tray with a rosebud in a vase and two slices of toast. Butter, jelly, and honey lay in a little bowl. The tray also held a cup and a tea pitcher with a flowered cozy on top. "I wrote down my personal number on a card. Feel free to call me any time day or night. Since I live on the premises, I can be here in just a few minutes."

Joy smiled. "I see God in your eyes, Ramona."

"What a lovely thing to say. God speaks to us in many ways. And if you want to read God's words, there's a Bible in the top drawer of your dresser. I suggest reading something in the New Testament first—maybe the book of John."

"I'll do that. I feel better now."

"I will be at the front desk in the morning until I leave for church at a quarter till ten, so hope to see you then."

Joy stood and walked her friend to the door. "*Gracias* for everything, Ramona."

"*De nada.*"

BENIGNO stepped out of the shower that evening with a heart heavier than his steel-toed boots. His hopes had soared earlier at meeting a girl who made his heart race. Then they'd fallen back to earth at the sight of the un-tanned stripe on her ring finger.

A thought pinged in his brain, setting his heart to race again. He'd call Ramona to settle his question once and for all. She would understand, and would never steer him in the wrong direction.

"Hi, *Tia* Ro, it's your favorite nephew, Benigno."

A chuckle came across the line. "You are my only nephew who calls me *Tia* Ro."

"That's right, and your special nephew wants to stop by tomorrow afternoon if you will be home. I'd like to ask about visiting with one of your guests."

"Might this be my guest with the bright green eyes and lovely dark hair?"

"The same."

"But why would you ask me?"

"I admit I was attracted to her at first, but nixed that after I noticed a pale line on her ring finger. Where is her husband?"

Tia Ro's voice changed. "I will leave the details for her to tell you in her own time, but I assure you she is *not* married."

"Okay. You've got me intrigued now, and made me happy. I'll be there after church. I'm hoping she'll let me take her sightseeing. *Adios*."

I'm glad she's not married, but I still don't know what

caused her sadness.

JOY awoke at ten. She'd stayed up to read John until she drifted off after midnight. Such wonderful inspired words that lifted her heart. *Forgive me, Father, for failing to be consistent in my Bible reading these past few months.*

Too late to attend church with Ramona, so this would be her day to walk to the ocean.

Slipping on a bathing suit, cover up, and flip-flops, she grabbed a towel, and some sunscreen, then went out her back patio door. The roar of the waves and the salty tang of the ocean air reminded her of their last family vacation to Myrtle Beach, South Carolina, before her mother died. Such good memories—back when they'd been a happy family, a whole family. Or that was how it seemed to her nine-year-old self.

During her reading of John last night, she'd begun to ask God questions, so she continued their silent conversation on her short walk. *God, I love you. I don't understand why my mom had to die and leave me so alone, but I will trust You. Thank You for sending Ramona into my life to comfort me, and thank You for this gorgeous day. Help me to know more of You.*

The soft, warm sand massaged her feet. She found one of the beach chairs marked "Inn of the Dove," and placed her things on it, then turned and studied the vastness of the ocean and sky. The waves at the edge of the shore gave a lacy border to the gorgeous picture. From there, the water morphed into light gray, to aqua, then to a darker blue before it met the shimmering, light-blue horizon.

God had created every bit of this. It was all too marvelous for a human to think of and create. Ramona had said God called everyone. Could He be speaking to her in the sound of the ocean waves? *God, help me listen and hear Your voice again.*

She walked out into the waves up to her knees and listened to the roar of the surf, but that was the only sound she heard. Next she padded to the chair where she sunbathed for a few minutes, trying to listen again, then gave up and headed back to her room to shower.

When she finished, her stomach growled, so she dressed, then hurried to the kitchen area to see what she could grab for a late breakfast. Her eyes widened at the spread of sweet rolls, and juices, plus bacon, and eggs, and biscuits, and more in covered warming dishes. Ramona must go all out for Sundays.

Finding no one else in the room at the time, Joy stayed there to eat. In a few minutes she heard the screech of tires stopping. New arrivals?

Ramona and Marcos walked in. When Ramona spied Joy, she crossed the room and hugged her. "How are you this morning, *mi querida*?"

"Wonderful. Sorry I missed going with you this morning, but I stayed up late reading the whole book of John. Then I walked to the ocean before coming back to this feast. You treat your customers like family, Ramona."

"*Sí*, you are *mi familia*. I can tell you have a love for the ocean, and our beautiful country, and a heart like a true Puerto Rican."

"*Gracias*. I'm glad I'm staying two weeks, and I do plan to go to church with you next Sunday."

"Certainly. What do you want to do the rest of today?"

"I want to see more of Old San Juan, travel down some side streets, and maybe eat some of that ice cream or shaved ice you told me about."

The door opened again. A familiar voice called out, "*Tia* Ro, where are you?"

Ramona beamed. "In the kitchen, Benigno."

He hugged Ramona like he hadn't seen her in ages.

Joy stepped back, and tried to disappear to her own room. Ramona reached for her hand. "Joy, I believe you already met my nephew, Benigno." The owner's eyes twinkled. "Benigno, have you eaten yet?"

"No, *Tia* Ro, I came straight from church because I know what a feast you lay out each Sunday."

"Then eat already. Time is wasting. Joy wants to go sight-seeing in Old San Juan this afternoon." She turned to Joy. "Benigno told me he plans to go into the Old Town today, too, so I can think of no better person to escort you."

Joy shook her head. "I'll be fine touring on my own. I stayed out the other night until almost dark."

Benigno waved a finger in front of her face. "A gentleman does not let a lady sightsee alone. And I know lots more than the guidebooks can tell you since I've lived here all my life."

Her eyes narrowed. "I will only let you escort me if you allow me to pay for any meals." She lifted her chin in challenge, thinking he might refuse.

A grin graced his mouth. "*Sí*. I accept. He glanced down at her flip-flops. "May I suggest you wear some good walking shoes?"

"Yes, I'll go change while you eat." She turned to face Ramona. "Should I dress up or just go casual?"

"There will be people dressed in all fashions, so wear whatever you are most comfortable in."

Joy went down the hall, her heart thudding in her ear with each step she took. What had she agreed to—spending another day in Ben's company? Could this be an answer to prayer? Or not?

BENIGNO glanced up at *Tia* Ro while he ate. "When did you start adding matchmaker to your shingle?"

The corners of his aunt's mouth turned up. "Since I knew you wanted to ask her, I thought I would help get things started. The rest of the day is up to you. "

Benigno winked at her. "Thanks." He finished his plate, then eyed the dessert bar, and scooped up some of his *tia's* famous *Arroz con Dulce*. He also dished out another bowlful and set it next to him with a spoon and napkin.

Joy joined them dressed in white slacks, tennis shoes, and an aqua blouse with ruffles that reminded him of ocean waves—one of his favorite things. "Please sit and eat some of *Tia* Ro's *Arroz con Dulce* with me. She makes the best on the island."

Joy sat then took a few small bites while he finished his. "I know it's wonderful. I already ate my share earlier, and I love the creamy rice with the raisins and cinnamon. We'll have to walk extra to work off these calories, you know."

As if she needed to count calories. "No worries. The Old Town is one square mile that holds five hundred years of history, so it is impossible to see it all in one afternoon. We'll stroll through the neighborhood toward one of the forts, and you can stop me any time you see something you want to explore. Sound like a plan?"

"A great plan. Let's go." She stood and beckoned him to follow.

He would follow her anywhere. They'd known each other barely a day, but his heart was hers for the asking.

Chapter 4

JOY reveled in the ancient architecture and fascinating sounds as they walked through the Old Town of San Juan. Except for her cell phone in her pocket and the attire of the people milling around, she would have believed in time travel.

They stopped in front of a palatial white home. Ben pointed toward a sign that read '*La Casa Blanca* .' "This is one of the oldest buildings in the city. It will be five hundred years old in six years. Ponce de Leon built it in 1521."

Wow. "*The* Ponce de Leon I studied in history who searched for the Fountain of Youth?"

"The very same. He built this structure as a fortress and a home for his family before he left to explore further. His family resided in this house for two hundred years. Now it is a museum depicting life in the sixteenth century. Would you like to take the tour or keep walking?"

"I definitely want to do the tour, but I may come back to do that another day." She smiled at him and quirked an eyebrow. "When I don't have my own personal guide."

"I know you have a good eye for photography, so let's

go down this street." They turned at a sign pointing to the San Juan Gate.

The crowds thinned in this part of the city, and she could see a tall stone sculpture straight ahead. She walked around it, then stared at Ben. "What's this?"

"It's called *La Rogativa* , and commemorates a true story from 1797 when the British attacked Old San Juan. The people of the city knew they were outnumbered and facing defeat. A brave priest led a religious procession through the city anyway. When the British saw the crowd and thought reinforcements had slipped in, they left. The city was saved."

"How wonderful. Did you study all these stories in school?"

"Yes, and many more. We Puerto Ricans are very proud of our heritage and history."

Fascinated, she snapped shot after shot of the statue and the shadows the figurines made on the Plaza. As she moved around the figures, she startled at seeing water off the edge of the Plaza. She glanced at Ben with another question on her face as she turned to photograph it.

"That is the San Juan Bay, which wraps around this end of the island, making it a great spot for a fort. We still have a few hours of sunlight remaining, so I suggest when you finish here, we walk toward *El Morro* , one of the two forts guarding Old San Juan."

"I'm glad this is a digital camera or I would already be out of film. I could take pictures from this vantage point until dark, but I do want to see one of the forts today. I can come back later."

He crossed over onto a gravel path. "This will lead us up the hill to *El Morro* . Look off to the left, and you will see several good views of *Isla de Cabra*."

So many great shots all around. She snapped a dozen or more, and promised herself she'd come back here at various times of the day to get the different shades of blue on the water with the changing sunlight.

When they reached the gate for *El Morro* , Ben had his money out for their tickets.

"I should be buying the tickets."

"But you said you would buy our evening meal, and I am working up an appetite, so you better save your money for that." He winked.

She laughed out loud. The first time she'd laughed in over a week. "You are good medicine for me, Ben."

They spent the next two hours exploring the fort and its cannons, towers, the scary dungeon and the lighthouse. Another treasure trove of history. A site she knew she would want to see again.

Joy opened her backpack to pull out some water, but found none. "Where can we buy some bottled water?"

BENIGNO checked his watch. Almost five. "The fort closes at five on Sundays. There are stands outside the fort where we can purchase a drink or even a shaved ice."

"Ooh, that sounds refreshing. Ramona suggested shaved ice when I first arrived, but I haven't experienced it yet."

"The sun will be setting in less than two hours. A

photographer friend told me the best time to shoot the outside of the fort is at sunset. Do you want to find some shaved ice on the way to the field which has the best vantage point?"

"Almost sunset? Where has the day gone?"

"Time passes fast when you are enjoying yourself, no?"

"You're so right. Of course I want some sunset shots, if you have the time. You've been so kind to escort me here and share all these wonderful scenes with me."

"It has been my pleasure to watch your enjoyment, and I do hope you will share with me some of your pictures."

"Of course." She looped her camera cord around her neck. "Lead on to the shaved ice stand."

When they found it, she insisted on paying. "What's your favorite flavor?"

"Probably coconut, but I'm partial to cherry also. I think I'll have those two flavors swirled together." He ordered one from the woman behind the stand.

"Me too. And a couple bottles of water." She handed the woman a five and a few dollar bills, glad she didn't have to learn a new currency on this trip.

As the first bite touched her tongue, she moaned. "How have I lived my whole life without a coconut and cherry shaved ice?"

He laughed, her delight pleasing him. "It does hit the spot on a warm day." Nodding at a field of flowers, he walked toward it. "Let's rehydrate while we walk to the field to see where you want to photograph the sunset."

They ate while they walked several hundred yards, then

found a trash can and threw their paper cones away. Joy held her camera up to her eye while trying several different angles of the fort. Then, as the sky glowed pink and orange, she snapped in earnest, moving from one side of the field to the other and back again. The sky morphed to purple with pink streaks, and she clicked even faster for a few more minutes.

She huffed out a sigh. "The lighting didn't last long. I'm glad I have twelve more days in Puerto Rico. But that won't be enough to take all the photo opportunities I've seen today."

He chuckled. "Maybe you could stay longer or come back again." *I certainly hope she will.*

"Maybe." She put her lens cover on. "Where to now?

"I don't know about you, but the shaved ice whetted my appetite for some real food. Ready to go to dinner?"

"*Sí* , I am famished, too. We really did walk off all that brunch we ate at Ramona's."

"Do you like Puerto Rican food?"

"Yes. I love Ramona's cooking and the *Mofongo* I ate the day I arrived. "

"Then I know just the place. One of my favorite restaurants with authentic Island cuisine is *La Mallorquina* , on San Justo, right off Fortaleza Street." He reached for her hand. "So we don't get separated. The crowds always increase after sunset."

WARMTH spreading through her, Joy allowed Ben to

hold her hand. Her closeness to him confused her. Ricky hadn't held her hand much at all, although she'd often wished he would. Here she was in Puerto Rico with a man she'd known less than two days, feeling comfortable and safe holding his hand.

Ben showed her the street sign for Fortaleza. "So you can find your way back to our 'restaurant row' another day."

They walked a few more blocks before coming to *La Mallorquina* , a stately building painted burnt orange with black doors outlined in white.

A hostess seated them at a table for two set with a linen cloth and two leather bound menus atop their place settings of china. Crystal and silverware sparkled in the light of the chandelier. "Your waiter, Pablo, will be here to take your order after you have time to peruse the menu."

After studying the menu, Joy glanced at Ben. "I knew a little Spanish before my trip, and have learned a few more words since I arrived, but I'm not prepared to read a whole menu in Spanish."

"No problem. I can interpret it for you. I already know what I'll order—*Asopao*. It's a hearty stew made with fish and shellfish. They make the most authentic on the Island, as good as *Tia* Ro's."

She smiled. "That reminds me, I know *Tia* means aunt, so how is Ramona your aunt?"

"She is my mother's older sister."

"And why do you call her *Tia* Ro?"

"My father left us to go back to America when I turned two. I don't have any memories of him except for a few pictures. My *tia* took us in to live with her, and her husband,

and Marcos in their small apartment. I couldn't pronounce Ramona, so always called her Ro. She acted like another parent to me, and Marcos treated me like his little brother, so we have stayed close even after we moved out several years later."

"I see." *He must have inherited his blue eyes from his American father.* "So you are an only child like me?"

"*Sí* , except for Marcos."

The waiter stopped by. "Are you ready to order, or do you need more time?"

Benigno fastened his eyes on her. "Would you like to try the *Asopao* ? Or I can read you some more items."

"I like stew and seafood, so I'll try the *Asopao* ." She closed her menu and waited until the waiter left to share more about her family. "My Mom died when I was ten, so I grew up with only one parent, too."

"I got pretty lonely sometimes, did you?"

"Yes, my Dad is very quiet, so I spent a lot of time in my room alone reading, which helped me do well in school."

"I also spent the afternoons alone in my room reading until my mother came home from work. And it did make me a better student than many of my friends. As my mother always said, "Look at it as the rainbow after the rain. What we see as painful, God can use for good.""

She nodded, but couldn't decide if she fully believed that or not.

When their salads came, Ben reached for her hand, and said a short prayer. Her hand tingled even after he released it.

ALMOST finished eating, Ben drew in a fortifying breath. Time to bring up the question he'd been waiting all day to ask. "I noticed the white band on your ring finger yesterday, so I called *Tia* Ro last night. I wanted to ask you out, but not if you were married or engaged." He paused, hoping she would look at him. When she didn't, he continued. "She said you weren't married, but I would have to let you tell me the details."

She raised her head, the dread in her eyes evident. "Can we leave and talk about this in private?"

"Of course. Do you wish to order dessert?"

"No, everything tasted delicious, but I'm already full."

"Let's find a place to talk, then we can return to *Tia* Ro's and eat one of her desserts."

She nodded.

When the waiter returned with the check, Ben slid the tray over to her. This was not the time to argue about who paid.

They walked back to the entrance to the Old City, and he hailed a taxi. He wouldn't broach the ring issue until they were alone again. Instead, he pointed out several places she might want to visit later like the brightly lit *El Capitolio* .

Glancing out the window, he spoke. "We're only a few blocks from the Inn. How about getting out of the cab to take a moonlit walk and talk on the beach? It's often private by this time of night."

"Okay."

Just what he wanted to hear.

JOY shivered as they reached the beach. "This is the first time I've been cool since I arrived."

He put his arm around her shoulder. "It's the Trade Winds. See the clouds covering the moon? It will probably rain tomorrow."

"So you're a weatherman, too?"

"We guides have to be able to read the weather. The responsibility for the safety of those under our care on the tours rests on our shoulders, so we have to watch for signs of storms to know when to get them to shelter."

And he has such nice broad shoulders to give shelter.

They walked in silence a few moments, and she listened to the waves again. Would she hear God's voice this time? Would He tell her how to explain her messed up life to Ben?

Joy's mind warred about where to start. Might as well get it all out and tell how stupid she'd been. Then he'd never want to see her again. She shuddered, and his arm tightened around her. "I got engaged six months ago to a guy I'd been dating for over a year. This trip was supposed to be our honeymoon."

She slipped away from him and walked toward the waves.

He followed and grabbed her hand. She needed his strength, so let it stay. "I guess I just don't know how to read men. I told you what a silent type my dad is. I never grew up comfortable chatting with guys, or dating long-term, until a friend from church introduced me to Ricky, her husband's brother. He wouldn't go to church with me, but she said he'd probably come around later like her husband did. He didn't. But he did pay attention to me and take me places, and I had starved so long for male attention, I stuck with it, thinking he must love me."

"Did he ever say he loved you?"

"Not at first, but later on when he wanted to get an apartment together to save us both on rent, he said he thought he was falling in love with me. I told him it went against my beliefs to live together so guessed we'd have to get married first. He stared at me like I'd said something crazy, but then said, "I guess so." That's when I started making wedding plans, and I knew just where I wanted to come on our honeymoon—Puerto Rico."

"A great choice," Ben agreed.

"Yes. I made all the plans and paid for everything since I had moved back in with my dad by then. Ricky thought it fair since he paid all his rent and expenses on the place where we would live." She paused and took a breath. "A week before the wedding he came by the house and told me he'd made a mistake about being in love with me. He'd met someone who loved him enough to move in with him without getting married, so we were over. She planned to move in that weekend."

"So he was seeing her while engaged to you?"

"Apparently. I tried to get the ring off my finger to throw at him, but he laughed, and said to keep it since it was zirconia anyway." She cried, and he pulled her in close to him.

After a few minutes, her tears stopped, and she became

angry again, like she'd been the night of his betrayal. Angry at Ricky, and angry at herself for living in her own little happy, clueless world instead of the real world—a world where she didn't know how to read men, a world where men couldn't be trusted.

She yanked away from Ben. "I know you're just feeling pity for me, and probably never want to see me again, so please take me to the inn."

Ben stared at her, a confused look on his face. "Not at all. I'm thinking it's a good thing that guy's not here, or I could teach him a thing or two about how to treat a lady." He slammed a fist into his palm. Hard.

Joy chuckled at gentle Ben acting ferocious as a bear. "Sorry. No one's ever defended me like that before. I kind of like it."

"I'm glad, because you need to know you're worth it, Joy. I'm sorry you had to go through all this, but I'm not sorry you came to Puerto Rico. I want to get to know you better." He nodded toward some lights further away from the shoreline. "That's the back of Tia Ro's property. We can make our way inside now."

When Joy checked the clock in the kitchen, she couldn't believe it showed after eleven PM. "I'm sorry I kept you out so late. Don't you have to work tomorrow?"

"I do, but not until ten on Mondays, so don't worry about me getting my beauty sleep." He shot her a lopsided grin.

"Thank you again for such a wonderful day, especially for listening to me and defending me." She peered into his eyes. "I better go to bed and let you get home."

He held up a finger. "One more thing."

"Yes?"

"The next two days I'm scheduled to lead ziplining tours. Would you want to try that?"

Her stomach dropped to her toes at the idea. "No way. Sorry."

He chuckled. "That's okay. How about another rain forest tour on Wednesday?"

Should I go? The sights and sounds and scents of the rain forest flooded her memory. "Okay, Wednesday it is."

"Fine, I'll call Marcos tomorrow to set it up. Check with him on Tuesday. My treat."

"Will do. Thanks again." She walked down the hallway to her room.

When she turned, Ben still stood in the foyer. He waved.

Her fingers fluttered toward him before going into her room and shutting the door. Was the door to her heart opening a crack?

She readied for bed, but couldn't sleep for all the thoughts swarming in her head. Was Ben drawn to her? Was it too soon for her to be feeling attraction for someone else? Her heart couldn't stand to be blindsided again by a man.

A coqui chirped. She stilled. Was God trying to speak to her? She used to hear God speak to her heart, but hadn't heard Him for over six months...since the night she accepted the engagement ring from Ricky. Had God stopped speaking or had she stopped listening, afraid He might say He didn't want that marriage for her? Did she deserve to hear His voice when she had ignored it for her own desires?

Would she ever hear His voice again?

She turned and tossed until past midnight before falling asleep.

ON his way home, Benigno forced himself to concentrate on his driving instead of on the special woman who lived up to her name by bringing joy to his heart. He'd been happy for Marcos when he and Teresa had fallen in love, but he never thought it could happen to him—not this fast.

He relived the day from the moment he arrived at *Tia* Ro's house to his hours with Joy—holding hands in Old San Juan, and walking on a moonlit beach where she opened her heart to him. It played before him like a dream. If so, he didn't want to awaken.

Parking in front of his small condo, he sat in the car and recalled her green eyes with the gold flecks shining in the moonlight as they walked on the beach.

How could he wait until Wednesday to see her again? *I've got it bad.*

He went inside and fixed a glass of milk and crackers, the same snack his mother always fed him when he was hungry at night. His mom and Joy would love each other. They were both so important to him, how could they not?

That decided, and his stomach full, he fell asleep.

The next morning on his way to *El Yunque*, he called Marcos.

"Hey cuz, have a good weekend with Teresa?"

"Great. I hope you get to find out how wonderful it can

be someday."

"Me too. I told Joy last night that I wanted to take her on another Rain forest tour so she can shoot more pictures. The next time I'm scheduled to do that tour is Wednesday morning, so could you arrange to bring her and any other guests who want to go that morning? Around ten as usual?

"Sure. I'll check with *Mamá* about other guests, and let you know, but I'll bring Joy either way. So you all hit it off yesterday?"

"I think so, at least I hope so."

Marcos laughed. "Sounds like you've got it pretty bad."

"Maybe. I appreciate you bringing her over. See you Wednesday."

Glad he had two full days of tours to keep him occupied, Ben focused on his day ahead. How would he occupy his long, lonely evenings?

Chapter 5

MONDAY morning, Joy slept until nine. Must be cloudy. Ben had predicted rain for today. Why had she thought about Ben so early?

Better hurry and get dressed, or she might miss breakfast, although Ramona always had something available.

Joy slipped flip flops on with her Bermuda shorts and top, then went to eat.

She gladdened at finding Ramona sitting at the kitchen table with a pile of folded napkins. "How nice to have some company for my late breakfast."

The older woman smiled. "How late did Benigno keep you out last night?"

"After eleven. He said he didn't have to go into work until ten today." Joy lifted a sweet roll from the serving plate, added some grapes to her dish, then poured a glass of juice before sitting down across from her host.

Ramona raised an eyebrow. "You must have enjoyed yourselves to stay out so late."

"The day went so fast. I didn't get to see half the things I wanted to, so I plan to go back later." She glanced out at the rain hitting the glass doors. "Probably not today."

"It doesn't usually rain all day in Puerto Rico, so you could go this afternoon if it clears off. But I am always thankful for the rain to beautify our island."

Conviction stole over Joy. That's one big difference between me and Ramona. She's always thankful for whatever happens. "Have you always been so grateful and trusting of God, Ramona?"

The owner's honest eyes searched Joy's. "I make the choice each morning to trust God and be grateful for His answers to my prayers, even if His answer is no."

Joy pondered the words. Had she ever thanked God for a prayer He answered with no? No, she'd been too selfish, wanting her own way, no matter what. "I don't think I've ever thanked God for an unanswered prayer."

"I believe God always answers our prayers. Sometimes the answer is yes, sometimes maybe or wait, and sometimes the answer is a big no. For our own good."

"I can see the truth of that now." Joy nodded. "How did you get so wise?"

Her host stood and walked over to the coffee pot. "That story will take another cup or two of coffee, *mi amiga*. Do you have time?"

Joy waved her hand toward the rain hitting the windows. "I have the time if you do."

Ramona sat down and stirred her drink.

The swirling liquid in the cup reminded Joy of her life going around in circles and getting nowhere. "I can't think of anything better for me to hear on this rainy day than how to listen to and trust God."

"*Sí*, it is the most important thing we ever learn. And one we often don't see the need for until we go through hard circumstances."

Like my breakup. "I see what you mean."

"As a young woman, I believed in Christ, but didn't give Him the Lordship He desired and deserved. I married Pedro and we had Marcos a couple years later. We loved visiting in Old San Juan and wanted to buy some property here and run a business together. That sounded better than going to work separately and only seeing each other and Marcos for a few hours in the evenings and on weekends. We didn't go out much, just took walking trips around the Old Town. The day we saw this inn on one of our jaunts, we both knew it was where we were meant to be."

"So, you bought it and lived happily ever after?"

"No, that only happens in fairy tales." Ramona sighed. "We put in a low bid, because we knew it would take a lot of work and material. Someone else bid higher, and we mourned the loss of this inn like a death in the family. We kept walking, but took side streets to avoid going past it. We kept saving, and a year later, someone told us it was for sale again. The first owner had gone bankrupt trying to make all the repairs. The building and grounds were in worse shape than before with many half finished projects. Pedro spent hours calculating how much it would take in material alone. He bartered with our family and friends to do the labor." She stared out into space as if seeing it all happen again.

Joy couldn't wait to hear the rest of the story. "You bought it this time?"

"Yes, we did, and God supplied the labor and funds each time we needed it. He also supplied the initial furnishings when a motel several miles away went out of business, and we were able to buy everything there for pennies on the dollar."

"God rewarded your trust in Him."

"No. We were still trusting in ourselves and what we could do. We spent a year fixing it up, and finally moved in when Marcos turned fourteen. My Pedro and I spent one happy, busy year running the Inn of the Dove together."

"He was nine years older, but neither of us worried when he woke up with chest pains early one morning. He blamed it on indigestion. I finally convinced him to let a neighbor drive him to the hospital. After several hours of waiting, a doctor came out and told me my husband had died of a heart attack at the age of forty-five."

Joy covered her new friend's hand with her own. "I'm so sorry. What a shock that must have been."

Ramona wiped away her tears with a tissue. "Of course, but the greatest shock came when I found out he had taken out a second mortgage on the inn to cover the months we couldn't make the payments. I guess he didn't tell me because he didn't want me to worry. His insurance barely covered the funeral and burial, and I didn't know how I would make the payment each month. I had to find a way to keep the home and business Pedro and I shared. I prayed, and begged God, and made promises to Him, but He remained silent."

"How old was Marcos?"

"Fifteen, almost a man, and when I told him we might lose the inn, he wanted to quit school and go to work full time. I insisted he stay and at least graduate high school. He already helped so much around here, as he still does."

They sat silently a couple minutes before Joy asked, "But you are here now, and your inn is top-notch, so how did it all work out?"

"Only by the grace of God and a lot of hard work. You know from your job in the travel industry that our high season here is from December until April. Plus, we can count on Puerto Ricans booking in July during our many festivals. The other six months our rooms were often half empty, but we still had to pay all the monthly expenses."

Joy nodded. "Yes, that's the travel industry in a nutshell."

"Every Monday after my husband died, I fasted and prayed for God to show me a way to keep the inn without Marcos having to quit school. Each time I prayed our Lord's prayer, 'not my will, but Thine,' and surrendered it all to Him. I told Him I would obey Him, whether He gave me the answer I wanted or not.

Two months after Pedro's funeral our minister pulled me aside at the end of church on Sunday morning. He said a Christian organization in the States had contacted him about holding marriage conferences in Puerto Rico during the low-season months of May and June for ministers and their wives. The organization wanted a wholesome place near many of the tourist areas so the couples would be able to sightsee on their own when they weren't in classes. They planned to book twenty rooms per week during those two months. I agreed to house at a discount the scouting team of five couples who would be bringing their own wives."

"They chose the Inn of the Dove for their lodging?"

"Yes, they did, and still do. I had one month to get ready for them. Juanita and other members of our church spent all their spare time helping me spruce up the inn, and our nearby church agreed to rent them the needed classrooms. After their week here, all the minister's wives told their husbands they had to book our place, and bring them back for the conference, too."

"Wow! What an answer to prayer."

"Amen. After five years, the program had become so popular they needed more rooms. I suggested a few other inns, then one of the wives came up with the idea of holding the conference twice a year. I told them I would be able to do the months of August and September also at the low-season rate. So now I house many Christian couples for four months a year, and have always been able to make the mortgage payments and the needed upkeep and repairs."

"God answered your prayer the way you wanted after you fasted and prayed?"

"Yes, but it was much more than that. I had to come to the point of total surrender, giving up what I wanted, and being willing to accept whatever He wanted, even if it meant losing the inn."

Joy had some thinking and praying she needed to do. She stood and gave Ramona a hug around the neck. "Thank you so much for sharing your story with me. I think I'll lie down to rest in hopes of going sightseeing in Old San Juan again later."

Ramona smiled. "I will be praying for you, *mi querida*. You will hear His voice if you listen with an open, surrendered heart."

As she walked down the corridor to her room, Joy's eyes

filled with tears. Entering, she dropped to the floor and spilled out her heart.

God, forgive me for wanting my own way so much I didn't want to listen to You about my wedding plans because I was afraid You might say no. I realize now You were trying to save me from all this heartache. Help me to hear Your voice again, and listen and obey. I do want to surrender all. Please show me how.

After several minutes, she rose and went out to the patio to sit and drink in more of God's beauty. Would He speak to her here?

AFTER the rain abated, Joy stopped by the front desk on her way out. "I'm headed to the heart of the old town, Ramona. Do you have any advice for me since I'll be on my own today?"

"*Sí*, you will need to take a bus or cab to Pier One where the cruise ships dock, then go across the street to the Visitors' Center where you can pick up a self-guided tour pamphlet. That will help you decide where you want to go. You might also ask in the Center for a list of the art galleries in the Old City."

"That's a great idea. Thanks, Ramona." Joy hitched her backpack and camera onto her shoulder, snugged her wide-brimmed hat on her head, and went in search of a cab. She chanced upon a street vendor with chicken on a stick and purchased two of them to eat on her way.

After arriving at the Visitors' Center, Joy enjoyed the air

conditioning and the art work exhibited around the walls. She found a brochure for the walking tour and asked about the art galleries.

Surprised to find out the Old City contained over twenty galleries, Joy decided to concentrate on them today. The hardest to find turned out to be her favorite—*Galleria Sin Titulo*. It held a wide variety of artwork, including a photography section that she spent most of the afternoon exploring. Many of the photos were of San Juan, and some showed scenes she'd taken the day before. The contrast between her pictures and the ones here revealed how much she had to learn about photography.

She also loved *Galleria Botello*, both the art and the atmosphere. The building housed sculptures, and artwork ranging from historical to modern, with lithographs, linocuts, and also carvings. After filling her soul with the art, she sat on the patio and drank a bottle of water while she listened to the symphony of the gurgling fountain. Peace and gratefulness filled her as she closed her eyes. Lifting up a prayer to the Creator of beauty, she worshiped Him.

When she stepped outside, the sky had taken on the purple and pinks of the sunset from the night before, so she walked until she found a cab to take her back to the Inn.

In the lobby, Ramona greeted her with a big smile. "My shift just ended, so I hoped you would return before I left. I always like to make sure my single guests are in safely."

"I feel very safe in Old San Juan."

"Me too, but we mother hens sleep better when our *chicas* are under our wing."

Joy laughed. "I like being called your *chica*, Ramona."

"Good, let's sit and chat awhile with a soft drink and you can tell me about everything you saw."

"I can't imagine a better way to end my day."

MONDAY evening, Benigno sat on the couch flipping through the channels on the TV. He finally switched it off. Nothing held his interest—except a stunning young American woman. *I wonder how she spent her day. And her evening. Wish we could have spent it together.*

Sunday afternoon had flown by. Today had moved as slow as an iceberg. He'd never seen one, but he'd read that in one of his travel books.

Joy liked to travel as much as he did. Now that he had his degree and job, what held him back from seeing the countries he wanted to visit? Puerto Rico would always be his home, but he had two weeks of vacation he could use to go wherever he wanted.

His gut sank as the reason came to him. What fun would it be to travel to other sites without someone to share the experiences?

Turning the television back on, he scrolled to the travel channel. This would have to be his traveling companion for now.

He enjoyed a program about Spain. That country and Italy had topped his list for years. He figured if he went to Spain he could at least understand the language. Maybe he'd take a class in Italian to prepare for a trip there, too.

When the show ended, he turned the TV off for good.

After a shower, he pulled his Bible off the nightstand to read a Psalm, his nightly custom.

After reading Psalm thirty-seven halfway through, he went back to apply each verse to his life. *Dear Father, You know I don't fret or envy evil doers, but do trust in You and try to do good. I thank You for the safe place You let me dwell. I do delight in You, so I believe You will give me the desires of my heart—what You know is best for me. You know I am interested in knowing Joy better, but I commit my ways to Yours. I will be still and wait patiently for You...*

Benigno climbed beneath the covers, and lay still asking God to help him not to run ahead, but to delight even more in Him, and to give his heart the very desires He wanted for him. He asked for strength to continue to wait on His Spirit's direction. He listened until he drifted off into a peaceful slumber.

CHAPTER 6

Chapter 6

TUESDAY morning on Joy's way to breakfast, Marcos greeted her. "*Señorita* Worth, my cousin Benigno asked me to remind you about the tour tomorrow morning. Like last time, we will leave at nine and return around five. There is a newly-arrived couple who wish to go also. Does this work with your plans?"

"*Sí*, I will eat and be ready by nine o'clock. *Gracias*."

"*De nada*. I am happy to be able to arrange this for you." His eyes twinkled as though he knew a secret.

"See you tomorrow morning." Joy walked into the breakfast area, then helped herself to some rolls and fruit, and sat down.

Ramona entered and joined her at the table. "Still planning to go to the Old Town again today?"

"Yes, I'll tour *El Capitolio* this morning, then take the Flavors of San Juan walking tour at 4:30."

"I've never taken that tour, but other guests have told me it's loads of fun and tons of great food."

"I bet if you opened a restaurant, you'd be on the tour,

Ramona."

"*Gracias*, but I am happy running the inn. I get to be more involved in people's lives this way."

Joy gave her friend a hug. "And you do a great job of it, too. By the way, I'm riding a bus to *El Capitolio* this morning, but will take a cab straight to the front door of the inn tonight, so don't worry or wait up for me."

"All right, my *chica*, but I will write down bus directions before you leave."

"*Gracias*, *Mamá* Ramona.

They laughed together.

Joy ate breakfast, then went to her room to collect her things.

When she returned, Ramona handed her a sheet of paper and an apple. "In case you get hungry this morning. I know you won't be hungry tonight."

Following Ramona's directions to the bus stop, Joy was soon off on another adventure. She saw the large white building Ben had recommended and got off at the next stop.

She climbed the steps and went through the metal detectors at a security point. When she reached the rotunda, Joy saw many people looking up in the air, and as she leaned back to see the exquisite artwork in the dome, amazement stole over her. It did rival the Vatican, and she read and gleaned much more about Puerto Rico's history.

After leaving the Capitol building, she walked up and down the winding streets hoping to find a souvenir for her dad and the other workers in her office. Seeing a sign that pointed to *San Cristobal*, another fort she'd planned to see, she followed that street to the entrance.

Joy paid her entry fee and received a map of the twenty-seven acre compound.

"You may take a tour or use the map to guide you around," the man at the gate suggested.

"I only have an hour to spend, so will wander around with my map."

"Ciertamente."

She read the information on the wall, and found that like many of the oldest sites in San Juan, the Spaniards built *San Cristobal* for their own use. She also learned that as late as World War Two the United States Army used it as a military base. Later, the United Nations declared it a World Heritage Site.

Such a long history. Joy walked around the outside perimeter of the Main Plaza, and took several shots of the Atlantic. She mused what a great place it would be to work where you could hear the ocean waves all day. Ramona's statement earlier that she had a heart like a true Puerto Rican with her love for God's ocean and its soothing sounds filled her head.

The ocean breezes blowing through Joy's hair confirmed the words. She loved this island where she was just a short distance from God's ocean and could hear and feel His breeze everywhere.

Next stop—the Flavors of San Juan Walking Tour. Joy met up with the group and its personable guide. They walked up and down the streets of old San Juan, and she learned more about its history. At each stop she said, "I must come back here and sample more of the food."

She took a cab home with a full stomach and full heart and anticipation of seeing Benigno the following morning.

BENIGNO sat at his kitchen table eating beans and rice. Even at work where he usually stayed super-focused, he'd found his mind wandering to the lovely Joy Worth, a woman he'd met only twice.

What caused such an attraction? He admitted her looks played a factor, but it was much more than that. Admiration for her spunk and sense of adventure had impressed him. And her delight in everything around her.

He cleaned up the kitchen, then parked in front of the television again. Another travel show, this one about France. Had Joy ever been there, or did she want to go? Maybe they could discuss that tomorrow. He would see her in a little over twelve hours. What would make the time pass more quickly?

A run around the neighborhood should do the trick. He ran the five-mile loop encircling the lake and the condo complex.

Now tired and sweaty, all he wanted to do was shower and go to sleep. Soon ready for bed, the open Bible on his nightstand reminded him he'd stopped in the middle of Psalm thirty-seven the previous night.

He finished the chapter then re-read verse twenty-three to meditate on before sleeping. "If the Lord delights in a man's way, He makes his steps firm."

Lord, I delight in You, and I know You delight in me.

Keep my steps firm on the path You have for me. Not my will, but Thine.

ANTICIPATION swelled his heart as Benigno hopped out of bed on Wednesday morning. This was the day the Lord had made, and the day he would see Joy again.

He grabbed a banana to eat on his drive to the Rain forest. The cafeteria would pack lunches for him and his tour guests. The rain forest tours always delighted him, and eagerness for this one to start filled him. Seeing Joy again would be a plus.

Stopping by the tour office, he found out Marcos was bringing another couple with Joy, and the ranger office had also scheduled a couple and their young son. A manageable group.

He met the family of three in the office, so the four of them were already waiting at five before nine when Marcos pulled up in the inn's van.

Benigno spotted his invited guest in the back of the van and waved at her.

She smiled and waved back. His face warmed.

As the other guests unloaded from the middle seat, he greeted them.

Marcos introduced the inn guests to Benigno, "I'd like you to meet Paul and Ginny Martin from Wisconsin." He waved toward Benigno. "And this is my cousin Benigno."

"I can see the resemblance," Ginny replied. "I'm sure

we're in good hands then."

Marcos scooted back into the van. "My cousin will bring you to the meeting point at four." He winked at Benigno then waved as the van moved onto the road.

Benigno introduced the three tourists waiting with him. "We also have Jack and Regina Simmons all the way from Canada, and their son Seth."

The two men shook hands, and the others nodded toward each other.

"Today's tour will start here at the Palo Colorado Visitors' Center." Benigno pointed toward the park sign and map. "Around lunchtime, we will enjoy a picnic and then spend some time at *La Mina* Falls before traveling up to the Big Tree Trailhead where Marco will pick you up. This is a reverse of how I usually give this tour." He glanced at Joy. He wanted to wink at her, but curbed his impulse.

She winked at him and grinned.

His face heated in surprise, but he loved it, and planned to tell her so.

JOY couldn't believe she had winked at the guy. She'd never done anything like that before.

Ben spoke to the group. "We'll begin with a short added attraction, the *Baño Grande*. Let's be on our way. Remember to keep me or someone else from our party in sight at all times."

The others followed him down the trail.

Joy brought up the rear.

Ben stopped and waved his arm. The water thundered. He raised his voice. "The *Baño Grande* is a large man-made pool built in the 1930s by damming of the river. My grandfather told me he swam in it as a boy, but that is no longer allowed. It does provide some pretty photo opportunities."

Joy agreed and shot several pictures as the group followed Ben around the roped-off walkway and over a bridge where they could see the waterfall.

Ben led them back across the road and onto the *La Mina* Trail. "The *La Mina* waterfall is not as grand, but it is more fun since you can swim in it."

Joy inched up closer to Ben. "Any good photo stops on this trail?"

His gaze met hers, his eyes twinkling. "Anything special you're looking for?"

"A coqui?"

"I wanna see one of those, too," Seth bounced on his toes. "We read about them in school."

"We might hear them rather than see them. And they're more likely to be out in the afternoon or evening when the sun isn't so bright, so I'll keep my eyes open for one and let you know."

"Thanks." The boy skipped ahead to join his parents, leaving Ben and Joy alone for a short while.

Ben turned. "I hoped I'd get a chance to talk to you today. I get off at four. Would you let me take you on a personal tour then eat supper with me before I drive you home?"

Joy's heart raced, and her brain ping-ponged. Could she ever learn to trust a man again? "May I let you know later—when I see how tired I am?"

A frown darkened his face. "Sure."

Sorry she had disappointed him, she touched his arm. "I'll change my answer to yes, as long as you promise to not let me keep you out as late as last Sunday night."

He grinned from ear to ear. "I promise. You just tell me what time you want to be back, and I'll make sure it happens."

She couldn't see anyone else in the group. "I think we better catch up to the others."

Ben walked faster, and she kept up with him until the group came into sight, then slowed down a little, so the others wouldn't make a connection between the two of them.

Pulling out her camera, she took pictures of several plants she remembered from the first tour, then caught up with Seth's mom. "You've got a bright boy there. How old is he?"

"Seven, almost eight. He's the one who talked us into this trip to Puerto Rico after his class studied it this past year. I got online, found out how kid-friendly it was, and booked it. It's lived up to its advertising, too."

Joy grinned. "It's my first trip here, but I plan to come back. I haven't even seen all of San Juan I want to see yet, much less the rest of the country."

"I know what you mean. We scheduled three days in San Juan and four days for the rest of the island, and it's not nearly enough time. Seth and I both have to be back in school on Monday morning, and Jack has to go to work that night. When do you go home to Chicago?"

"I have another ten days." Joy didn't mention the un-honeymoon. "But it's going by too fast, and I'm already dreading the thought of leaving. It must have to do with the tropical breezes blowing through the palm trees." *And the people.*

"Yes, and there are no rain forests in Chicago."

Joy laughed. "How true."

The group had stopped again, so they joined them.

Ben explained something else to Seth. Joy let the words slide away while she studied the man. So confident, but not cocky. Knowledgeable, but not over your head. Friendly, but not pushy. Had she ever met a man like him? Not that she could remember. Her heart speeded up. He'd asked her out for a private tour and supper.

She snapped lots more shots along the way. A few times she managed to get Ben at the edge of a picture without seeming to be focusing on him.

By the time they stopped for lunch the sun shone straight overhead, filtered by the rain forest canopy. She'd seen a pond back a few yards. While Ben unloaded the food, she backtracked to the pond to see if she could find the coqui they'd seen there.

Intent on her search, she startled at the snapping of a branch behind her.

"Looking for something?" Ben's voice calmed her.

"A coqui?"

A laugh shot from his mouth. "You are persistent." He sent her a sideways smile. "It's so sunny today I don't expect them out until dusk, but I hope we'll see one on our walk later."

"That's good. I'm getting hungry now, so let's go eat."

After she picked up her food, she sat with the other lady from the inn. "Hi, Ginny. We're almost neighbors back in the states. I'm from Chicago. What part of Wisconsin do you hail from?"

"Madison, only a couple hours away. It's a small world."

"Yes, it is."

"Especially here in Puerto Rico."

Joy nodded in agreement while she took a bite of cheese and crackers.

Seth came running toward the group. "My dad and I walked ahead on the trail a bit and heard some rushing water. Is there a stream near here?"

Ben smiled. "A stream and the waterfall. After we clean up here we can be there in a few minutes."

They cleared the area. Joy stuffed her apple in her backpack.

After gathering up the remaining food and the trash bag, Ben led them onto the trail again.

Seth ran ahead until his dad called him back.

"We've made good time, so we can stay at the waterfall over an hour if you all want," Ben said.

Seth pumped his fist in the air. "Oh, boy!"

They all walked faster as the sound of the water

multiplied.

Joy spotted the bridge up ahead where they'd taken a group picture with the falls in the background.

Ben halted. "Do we want to take pictures of the falls from the bridge or go on to the waterfall first?"

"The waterfall," Seth shouted.

The group chuckled.

"The waterfall it is." As they rounded a bend in the road, Ben held out his arm toward the water. "*Cascada La Mina*."

The timbre of his voice saying those musical words again sent goose bumps up Joy's arms. She pulled off her long pants and shirt to reveal a tank top and a pair of shorts, then slipped into her beach shoes.

Glad she'd come prepared, Joy waded into the chilly water until she reached the falls, then plunged into the spray. It almost took her breath away, but she didn't care. She was more in tune with nature than she could ever remember.

BENIGNO stared at the lovely woman under the falls, then reminded himself he had five others to watch, too. His gaze roamed over the whole group, but his mind remained on the one with whom he'd be eating in a few short hours. The one with dark hair that now sported a glossy sheen. The one he'd held hands with in the Old City. Could he think of a reason to hold her hand tonight?

He glanced at her again, and watched as she came up out of the water, graceful and effortless in one fluid motion. She made her way to a rock, then lifted herself up by her slender arms. After running fingers through her hair, she placed her arms behind her, and lifted her face to the sun.

Forcing his eyes back to his job, he spotted Seth surrounded by both parents, and the other couple with their arms around each other in the water. Would he ever have a wife with whom he could share special times like that? Special trips like this? A special love?

Thank You Lord, that just like You made Eve for Adam, You have made a special woman for me. Help me to follow Your lead.

The next time he glanced her way, she'd disappeared, so he searched for her among the dozen or so people in the pool of water. Not finding her there, his eyes roamed the area, until he spotted her walking on the trail toward him.

She approached, then cut off toward her pack and camera on the rock behind him. Of course, she wanted her camera, not him.

"I could have taken a picture of you in the water if you wanted." He'd stored hundreds of her in his mind's camera.

"No thanks, I hate pictures of myself." The statement floored him. How could she say that?

She lifted the camera. "I saw some huge pink flowers on the edge of the water beside the falls."

"Sounds like lotus blossoms. I've seen them over there before."

"Great. I've heard of them but never knew what they looked like. I'll go take that shot as soon as I snap the two families in the water. I can get their emails or phone numbers to send the pictures to them after I get home."

Home. Why did she have to remind him she'd be going back to the States in a little over a week?

Once she reached the others, he kept them all in sight at once. The other two ladies were nice, but Joy stood out. After waving good-bye to them, she gracefully picked her way over the rocks to where the lotus blossoms bloomed.

Her long legs bent to get closer to take a shot. When she rose, she glanced at him and smiled.

Had she sensed his eyes on her? He smiled, then turned his attention back to the pool of water formed by the falls and counted. All five of his charges seemed to be having a great, safe time. Switching his attention back to Joy, his heartbeat raced when he couldn't find her anywhere in the area.

After a glance back at the group, he sped off in search of Joy. Where could she be? She always kept in sight of the group.

Just ahead of him, her head popped up. She must have bent over again to get another picture.

He took a deep, calming breath, then moseyed up to her. "Did you find some more interesting shots?"

"Yes." Her green eyes gleamed with flecks of gold. "I saw this pretty canario flower like the one you showed me last time, so took several shots of it."

"I see. Beautiful." His gaze fixated on her.

She smiled and turned away. "How much longer do we have here?"

He glanced at his watch. *Almost two.* "Just a few minutes, so I better go warn the others to get out and dry off a bit. Meet me back at the tall rock in five, okay?"

"Sure."

Benigno sped back to the waterfall. Seth's mom was handing him a dry shirt. "*Hola!*" He stepped closer to the pool and yelled at the other couple as he pointed at his watch. "Time to start hiking again."

They waved in reply and walked toward the edge of the pool.

Seth ran up to him. "That was the favoritest part of my trip so far. I can't wait to tell my friends I swam in a waterfall!"

"That's right. And Joy took some pictures to prove it."

"Wow." He ran to Joy. "Did you take pictures of me swimming under the waterfall?"

"I sure did. Tell your parents to give me their phone number, and I'll send them a digital copy tonight."

The boy jogged back to his parents.

Benigno peered into her eyes again. Their green deepened in the shade. "You made him very happy." *As you made me happy when you agreed to eat with me tonight.*

Since the group had all assembled, he suggested they take a couple shots from the bridge. He took several of the tourists with Joy's camera, then asked Seth if he would take one of him with the group, too, with Benigno's small camera. At least he'd have a picture to remember her by after she left.

CHAPTER 7

Chapter 7

JOY lay in bed that evening reliving the hours she'd spent with Ben. They'd walked through the rain forest until dusk, and she finally got to snap some more pictures of a coqui. Next he'd driven her to a nice restaurant where they talked and ate, before taking her back to the inn where he again invited her to go for a moonlight walk.

She could get used to beach walks, and was learning to trust this guy. Their only disagreement happened when he tried to persuade her to come back to *El Yunque* another day to take the zip line tour. That would take more trust than she could ever hope to have.

Her night musings filled with dreams of Ben and his many talents. Charming. Handsome. Trustworthy. Made her laugh. Treated her with respect.

She awoke sometime early the next morning with tears in her eyes. In her dream Ben tried to persuade her to stay in Puerto Rico and go ziplining with him, but she'd boarded the airplane and watched him shrink away as the plane flew higher and higher.

When Joy went to breakfast, she wondered if she were

still dreaming when Ben appeared in the breakfast area chatting with Ramona.

The owner stood. "I will leave you two to talk." She winked at Ben as she left.

Joy approached the table.

Ben rose and pulled out a chair for her. "What can I get you for breakfast?"

"Just a cup of hot tea and plain toast." Her mind raced as she watched him fix her drink and toast the bread. *What is he doing here?*

He handed her the plate of toast and cup of tea, then returned to carry back coffee for himself. "Guess you're wondering what I'm doing here."

She raised an eyebrow as she took a bite of toast.

"I want to get to know you better, Joy, and since you'll be leaving in seven more days, I took a week's vacation I had saved up. I want to spend as much time as possible with you. I hope you won't get tired of me being around, but I'm here to be your personal tour guide for wherever you want to go on the island."

Her hand flew to her chest. "I…I don't know what to say."

"Say yes." He grinned, and her heart melted.

"Yes."

"Where did you plan to go today?"

"I thought maybe some of the art museums in San Juan, but you might not be interested in art."

"I love art. I like all forms of beauty." He wiggled his

eyebrows.

She laughed aloud.

"Go change into whatever you'll be comfortable in for art viewing. You may want to grab a light sweater as some places are air-conditioned."

She scampered down the hall, more excited than she'd been in—forever?

BENIGNO stood as she returned a few minutes later dressed in a black and white sundress, with a pink sweater tied over her shoulders, black flats, and a pink bow holding her bangs back. She resembled a delectable dessert from head to toe, with a cherry on top.

This might be the best vacation I've ever taken.

"Your carriage awaits, *señorita*." They walked out of the inn, and he opened the door of his white Honda.

As he pulled into traffic, he gave her a sideways glance. "I hope you have a list of the museums you wish to see. Some are devoted just to art, and several more have art and history combined."

"*Sí*. I've been studying my guide books and picked out a few that are in the same area since I thought I would be taking a bus and walking today."

"Where do you wish to start?"

"How about the Museum of Art of Puerto Rico?"

"*Museo de Arte de Puerto Rico*. A great place where you

can see many different eras of Puerto Rican art."

"You even sound like a tour guide." She touched his arm, sending a thrill straight to his heart.

He pulled into the parking lot for the museum, then hurried to open her door.

As they entered the museum, she insisted on paying their entrance fees, then studied the brochure she received. "I want to start on this floor to make sure I have time to see all the classics before branching into contemporary, okay?"

"We're here to see what you want."

They roamed up and down the halls and exhibits. She spent much of her time studying the older paintings and religious ones.

He spotted a water fountain, went for a drink, and also checked his watch. A little after noon. Retracing his steps to find Joy still staring at a painting of Mary and the Christ Child, he waited until she looked up. "It's almost one. Do you want to grab a bite to eat and maybe come back here? Our tickets are good all day."

"That sounds good. Where do you suggest?"

"We can walk to the *Plaza del Mercado* . It has several stores and food stands."

She beamed him a pretty white smile. "Lead on."

They strolled the few blocks. Each ordered a fruit smoothie and a sandwich on a stick, then walked and talked some more on their return to the museum.

On the way back, he steered her into the Sculpture Garden behind the museum.

As they approached the bridge over the Koi pond, she

stared at him in bewilderment. "Where did the city go?"

He chuckled. "This is one of my favorite interludes in San Juan, kind of a hidden outdoor museum." He opened his arms toward the trees and plants surrounded by sculptures.

"Amazing."

They spent almost an hour covering the two acres and its many forms of art. "Would you like to go back inside now, or try another museum? I'll warn you that most of them close at five."

"We better go on then. Another on my must-see list is the Museum of History, Anthropology and Art. Is that one too far?"

"Excellent choice, and it won't take long in the car. It isn't nearly so large, either. It's at the University of Puerto Rico, so you can see where I spent four years of my life."

"Another plus. Maybe we'll run into an old girlfriend."

He frowned. "Not a chance. I've dated when friends set me up, but never more than a couple times. You hold the record for most dates with me."

What a shock! She gave him a sweet smile. "I believe you, but why?"

They buckled in, and he drove off. "I had an epiphany the other night after you told me about the rat you dated. It reminded me of how badly my dad treated my mom. I didn't want to be treated that way, or ever treat someone else that way, so I decided I'd wait for the one God gave me."

"Wish I'd been as wise as you." Joy sighed. "My trip is half over, and I have so many sites I still want to visit, and others like the museum I'd love to see again."

"Sounds like you need a longer vacation." He chuckled. "Or you could always move here." *Like she would do that.* "Do you have any family besides your dad?"

"A few cousins, but we lost touch after Mom died. I would worry about Dad, though. He doesn't do much except work and sleep."

Time to change the subject. "This next museum is mainly Puerto Rican artists and history."

"Good. I really liked what I saw in the Old San Juan museums and art galleries."

A great morning segued into a great afternoon. She surprised him with her interest in the history of his country, his people. Funny. Even though he was half *Americano*, he'd never identified with his dad's people.

He took her to one of his favorite *restaurantes* for supper, then asked her to take another moonlit stroll, and she accepted.

As they walked, he reached for her hand. She didn't pull away. His heart boomed louder than the surf. "Are you up for a surprise tomorrow?"

Her eyes widened, but she nodded. "What will I need to wear?"

"Shorts, or Capris, and a T-shirt, and lots of waterproof sunscreen. Wear a bathing suit underneath, and beach shoes, and a hat. That should cover it. I'll take care of everything else. We need to leave at seven. It'll be worth it. Trust me."

JOY awoke at six the next morning, still musing over what the surprise might be. She did trust this guy, and hopped out of bed, eager to jump into the day.

She packed then re-checked her backpack to make sure she had all the things Ben had listed. After dressing in green Bermuda shorts, a yellow sleeveless top, and beach shoes, she walked down the hall.

Ramona sat behind the desk. "I've put out some pastries and fruit you can pack in a box for you and Ben to eat on your drive. And some 'to go' cups for tea and coffee."

"Any hints on where he's taking me?"

"I wouldn't want to spoil the surprise, but I guarantee you will enjoy it."

Joy had almost finished packing their breakfast when Ben appeared. He waved to Ramona. "Thanks for breakfast, *Tia* Ro." He smiled at Joy. "Ready to go?"

"Ready and eager to find out where you're taking me."

Grabbing her backpack and the breakfast box, he waved again to Ramona.

"Take care of her, Benigno."

"You know I will." He winked at Joy.

Her heart fluttered. She steadied the two hot cups of liquid.

He opened the car door for her, then placed the breakfast box at her feet before stowing her pack in the trunk.

Slipping into his seat, he stared at her. "Are you ready for an adventure?"

Dragonflies buzzed in her stomach. "Maybe. It depends.

It's not ziplining, is it?"

He frowned. "Don't you know I wouldn't push you to do anything you don't feel comfortable doing?"

Her eyes met his. "Yes, I do."

"Then sit back and enjoy the day. But first, you could hand me my coffee, *por favor*." He pulled out the cup holder between them.

She placed his coffee in the holder nearest him, then took a sip of her hot tea before setting it in a holder, too. Next she opened the breakfast box and pulled out a croissant with ham and cheese. "Are you ready for this?"

"No, I better get us out of the city traffic first. You go on and eat, though."

Taking a bite, she moaned. "This is so good, even if I did make it myself."

He laughed. "If it's that good, maybe you could share a bite."

Tearing off the other corner, she put it between his lips. Soft lips. "How's that?"

"Yummy, but I can wait for more. You eat the rest."

She grabbed a banana from the box. "Want a bite of this, too?"

"Sure."

After peeling it, she held it up to his mouth, and he took a big bite. "Somebody's hungry."

"Yep. If there's another banana in there, I think I could eat it and drive."

"Here, take this one, and I'll eat the apple I packed." She

pushed it toward him, then grabbed the apple and bit into it. "Do I at least get some clues? Have I ever heard of where we're going?"

"We can play twenty questions. And for the answer to the second question it'll have to be a maybe since I don't know what you've studied about our island." He grinned. "Now you have eighteen questions left."

"Okay, let's see…how long will it take us to drive there?"

"An hour and a half to two hours, depending on the traffic."

"So, it's on the coast?"

"Yes."

"East or west coast?"

"East."

They continued with this game until she used all her questions. By that time they were out of the city.

"May I have my sandwich now?"

"Now you get to play twenty questions. Yes, you may have your sandwich, and you now have nineteen questions you may ask."

He grinned. "*Touché*."

HE hadn't planned on this, but she told him he could ask twenty questions, so he would take advantage of it.

"What other countries have you traveled to besides Italy,

and now Puerto Rico?"

"Did I say personal questions?"

"You're out of questions, remember?"

She slapped her napkin on his arm. "I'll answer the ones that aren't too personal. I've been to Mexico and the Dominican Republic, and forty-eight of the fifty states."

"Wow."

"Remember, I work for a travel agency and get discounts."

"Which states have you not traveled to?"

"North Dakota and Montana. They're on my list for next year."

"So you've been to Hawaii and Alaska?"

"Good deduction. It's a shame you wasted a question on that."

"Very funny. Which of those did you like best?"

"Hawaii and its beaches, of course, but Alaska is amazing and different from any other state, not just in size, but the ruggedness of it, and the independent people."

"You're pretty independent."

She scrunched up her face. "That's not a question."

"No, but it's true."

She sat silent for several seconds. "Thank you." Then she turned her head to the window. "I had to be."

Not sure if she was looking at the scenery or taking a trip in her mind, he let her be.

Their game had passed the time, but he still had lots

more he wanted to learn about Joy. And a whole day to do that. He hoped she would try the snorkeling, but even if she didn't, there was still plenty to do on Icacos—swimming, beach walking, exploring, shell gathering, talking—maybe even staring into each other's eyes.

She flipped her hair around so fast it grazed his face. "I just saw a sign for Icacos. Is that where we're going?"

"You're out of questions, remember?"

She grinned. "Why else would we be on this road? I hope I'm right. Icacos was one of the places I read about, but didn't want to go alone."

"Your wish is my command."

"Oh good." She clapped her hands like a child. "I can't wait."

He made a left turn. "Only a few more minutes. Do you get seasick?"

"No, why?"

"We have to take a short water-taxi ride to the island. I packed some Dramamine just in case."

"You've thought of everything."

"I hope so."

She studied the shoreline until he stopped the car in the parking lot. No sight of Captain Stevie and his boat yet, but it was early.

"Ready to get out, or do you want to wait in the car?"

She unlatched her door and climbed out in answer. "This is gorgeous, and I can't believe I'm going to a private island in the Atlantic Ocean."

"Also known as the Caribbean Sea. We should be there in ten or fifteen minutes." Was that the rumble of a motor? Within a couple minutes, a yellow boat appeared on the horizon. "That's our ride." He waved.

Two people on board waved back. As they neared, Benigno could tell Stevie's wife, Becky, accompanied him.

Stevie hollered, "Land ahoy, matey."

Joy laughed. "Our captain is hilarious."

His friend had donned a pirate's patch across his eye and partially bald head. *Way to go, Stevie.*

Stevie pulled into the boat slip, and Becky tied his line off. They made a good team.

"Come aboard, mateys." Stevie extended his hand to Joy.

She glanced at Benigno. "I'll be right behind you all the way."

Joy gave the captain her hand.

Benigno steadied her as she jumped aboard, then he joined her. "Joy, meet two of my good friends, Becky and Stevie Villier. They moved here after he retired as a boat captain in New Orleans." He waved his hand toward his date. "Guys, I want you to meet my friend Joy."

Becky held out her hand to Joy. "Any friend of Benigno's is a friend of ours. Let me give you a tour of our boat."

As the ladies walked off, Stevie gave Benigno a thumb's up sign. "You did good, brother."

"I hope she thinks so."

The ladies rejoined them. As Stevie took the wheel, the

others gravitated toward the bow and watched as the boat bounced across the waves.

Captain Stevie used his microphone to announce, "Look to your right, and you can see the private island of Icacos, part of the Cordillera Keys Nature Reserve."

Benigno prayed Joy would enjoy the rest of the day and join him in an adventure.

Chapter 8

JOY donned her sunglasses and watched as the island grew larger and larger. She couldn't believe she was approaching this place she'd read about. Ben had made this dream come true for her. He was so sweet and considerate—a dream come true in many ways.

As the boat neared the island, it stopped, then turned around and backed up. Ben appeared at her side. "Ready to disembark?"

She gave him her hand. "Am I going to get wet?"

"Sometime today you might, but I can help you off the boat and keep you dry for now."

Becky hollered, "We can pick you up at three and drive to the other side of the island or come after you at four."

"Three sounds good. I think Joy will like seeing the wild side of the island."

Wild side? Joy shuddered.

Becky handed Ben a red cooler, Joy's backpack, a black bag that must be his, an umbrella, and some towels. Then they watched the couple leave. No one else in sight. This really was a private island.

Joy studied Ben as he carried the cooler behind the shade of a large rock, then arranged the other supplies.

"Were you a Boy Scout?"

"Why?"

"You're always prepared."

"I hope so. What would you like to do first—beachcomb for shells, go for a walk, or swim, sunbathe, or explore the island?"

So many options. "Let's walk along the beach, and maybe I'll gather some shells as a memento of this trip."

"Sounds good. Let's stow our gear behind that rock with the cooler and I'll grab a mesh bag for your shells. I've never had anything stolen out here, but would hate for this to be the first time."

She carried the towels while he hid the backpacks. He produced a bag. "Let's walk toward the sun now, then when we turn, it won't seem so hot on the way back."

"How many times have you been here?"

"Lots. Maybe close to a hundred. It's a summertime hangout for young people."

"But it's always warm here, so why not in the wintertime?"

"We do come here on weekends even then, but the days are shorter in the winter, and many young people are in school then."

Of course. She stooped to pick up several shells along the way.

He held out an interesting looking one. "It has the tip broken off, unique in its own way."

"I agree. I'm learning we're all broken in some way, but God sees us as perfect."

"You're so right."

They walked a little further then turned around. It did feel cooler this way, with the sun at their back and the breeze in their faces. Heavenly. And perfect company on a perfect day.

When they reached their spot, Ben walked to the cooler and produced two cold bottles of Coco Rico. "Ready for a drink?"

"Sure." She reached for a bottle, but he pulled it back. "Something I need to tell you first. There are no facilities on this island, so the more you drink, the more you'll need to visit the bushes with the roll of toilet paper I brought."

She held out her hand. "Coco Ricos are worth a trip to the bushes."

HE laughed. A girl after my own heart .

"We have Icacos to ourselves this morning, which is why I wanted to arrive early, before the snorkeling boats arrive around ten thirty. They park and snorkel for an hour or two before leaving. Then we should have it all to ourselves again."

"What will we do while they're here?"

"If you want to snorkel, I'd rather do it later without a

crowd, but we can sunbathe and then eat an early lunch. This is your day, remember."

"Okay, let's walk the other way until the boats arrive, then we'll hurry back and sunbathe. I even packed a book just in case."

"Were you a Girl Scout?"

Her mouth drooped. "Just a Brownie. My mom was my leader until she got sick…"

"Sorry. I didn't know. Why don't you tell me the happy parts you remember about your mom while we walk."

She grabbed her shell bag and then turned to the right. "I'd like that. She was such a fun person. Everyone loved her, especially kids. She taught my Sunday School class and Brownies. She always dressed up for Halloween. Sometimes we even dressed alike. One year she made herself a tall purple crayon costume, and me a short one. Another year she played the scullery maid Cinderella, and I dressed up like Cinderella at the ball."

He laughed. "I would have loved to see that."

"I don't have many pictures of her, but I can show you the one I always carry with me when we get back to the inn."

"I'd like that."

At the hum of another boat motor, they turned and walked back to their spot.

He spread out the towels, brought her another drink along with her backpack, then went back for his own drink and pack.

She pulled out her latest Kim Vogel Sawyer novel and

started reading, soon lost in the world of a Mennonite girl. Such a simpler life. One she often envied.

Benigno watched the crowd jump off the snorkel boat into the water. They acted pretty tame, but he'd still keep an eye on them while pretending to read. Most of them just wanted to spend their time snorkeling, so they shouldn't be any trouble. But better alert than sorry.

He glanced at Joy, who had read a chunk of her book already. "Are you getting hungry yet?"

"Yes, and I need to visit the bushes." She held up her second empty Coco Rico with a grimace.

"No problem. I already scouted out a place not too far from the rock. I'll stand guard—a respectable distance away." He shook out his towel, and she did the same.

They stowed their belongings behind the rock again, and he grabbed the toilet paper and a shovel.

Keeping the rock and their stuff in sight, he led her over a hill and pointed to another rock down the hill twenty or so feet. "Go behind that rock, and I'll stay up here and watch our stuff." He handed her the roll of toilet paper and the shovel. "You can scoop some dry sand over the wet sand."

She giggled. "You're definitely prepared. Be right back." She glanced at him before she went behind the rock. He waved, then turned around toward the ocean.

A couple minutes later shuffling sand told him she neared. She handed him the TP and shovel. "Next?"

He grinned. "I think I can wait until this group leaves. Let's go see what I packed for our lunch."

They walked together down the hill. "Let's stay behind this rock. I don't have enough Coco Ricos for the whole group."

He opened his cooler to reveal fruit kabobs on skewers, sub sandwiches, chips and another container with a lid.

"What's in that?"

"You have to eat your lunch to find out. It's a special dessert for a special gal."

She bent over to open her sandwich.

He reached for her hand, loving the way it fit in his. "Let's pray. Father, I thank You for this beauty that surrounds us, and for this food to nourish our bodies. Lead us in Your paths, O God, today and always. In Your Son's name, Amen."

SUCH *a sweet prayer. Such a sweet man.* Joy lifted her head and took a bite of her sandwich. "Delicious. And the kabobs look almost too good to eat, but I won't let that stop me."

"Me either."

They ate in silence until the boat motor started again, and he peeked around the edge of the rock. "They're leaving. All ten of them."

"You counted?"

"How else could I make sure they all left?"

She laughed, but her heart warmed at his protectiveness. "I'm full. Do you want the rest of my chips?"

"Sure. I guess you'll never know what's in the container,

then."

She stuffed the handful of chips into her mouth then washed them down with another swig of Coco Rico. "Ready."

He chuckled while opening the lidded bowl to reveal some *Arroz con Dulce*.

"From Ramona?"

"Of course."

They ate the rich pudding with delight.

He took a last bite and drink before checking his watch. "We've got almost two hours until they return, so what would you like to do next?"

"How about exploring this side of the island a bit before we drive around to the wild side?"

"No snorkeling for you?"

"Not today, maybe next time. But I'd be happy to watch if you want to snorkel."

"It's more fun with a friend, so I'll wait until that next time."

They explored, first near the coast, then a little further inland. She saw some plants she'd only seen in pictures before, and some others she'd never even heard of.

Ben kept his eye on the time. "It's almost two thirty, so we'd better head back."

Stevie and Bec were on shore when they arrived. Ben hollered, "Sorry if you had to wait long."

"No worries. We came early for our own little beach walk." Stevie winked. "Let's assist the girls onto the boat, then I'll help you load up your things."

They did, and were soon on their way. The waters on the back side of Icacos were even more colorful than what she had seen so far—blues, greens, and shades of aquamarine she'd never seen before. It was hard to tell where the sky ended and the water began.

"What a fabulous day." Joy peered over at Becky on the boat chair beside her.

Becky raised her glass of iced tea in a salute. "It's a true paradise, huh? How much longer can you stay?"

"I leave next Friday morning, so less than a week now." Joy let out a sigh. "Wish I could stay longer."

"Why don't you?"

"I'd love to, except my dad would be all alone, and he doesn't have many friends."

"So invite him to come visit you here. We've invited all our family to fly down next Thanksgiving for a very thankful time together."

"I wish…"

"If you really mean that, give wings to your wishes."

Joy remained silent most of the way home, praying about how she could put wings on her wishes without hurting her dad.

ALMOST midnight, and Benigno couldn't fall asleep Friday night. What could've gone wrong? Joy acted like she'd had a super day until they got in the car to return. She hardly talked, just stared out the window and even closed her eyes for much of the trip. Was she sleeping or praying or what?

His brain wouldn't still until he pulled the Bible off his stand and read one of the favorite verses that always calmed him—Habakkuk 2:20 "The Lord is in His holy temple; let all the earth be silent before Him."

Mind silent, body silent, soul silent before God, he fell into a sound sleep.

Saturday morning Beningo couldn't wait to talk to Joy, so he phoned her at the inn. Ramona answered and reported Joy had gone out early, but hadn't said where. He'd told her he wanted to take her out to celebrate her last Saturday night in Old San Juan. Surely she wouldn't forget to be ready by five.

He ran around the condo complex and pond again, returned to shower, then drove over to his mother's. He hadn't seen her since church last Sunday, and couldn't wait to tell her about Joy.

Sitting in front of the small blue house where he'd grown up, memories flooded his brain. His mom's happy face the day she put a down payment on this place; his loneliness while she worked; the special evenings they had just the two of them, like their Saturday nights of popcorn and a movie; her letting him drive home the day he got his driving permit; her encouragement and proud smile the first day he left for college classes, then later at his graduation.

She'd done it on her own, and on a strict budget, and still worked hard to pay off the house before she retired. He couldn't have asked for a better example of a good work ethic or a Christian woman.

Joy reminded him of his mother, not in looks, but in her spunk to get things done. Together, they would be an unstoppable force.

Mom came out the front door with her watering can in hand. "Benigno, what are you doing out there?"

"Coming to see you, Momma." His childhood name for her. With a big hug he swung her off her feet.

"Put me down and come inside. I just took some of those banana muffins you like out of the oven."

"Yum. I must have smelled them all the way to my house." He wrapped his arm around her as they walked inside.

She laughed as she placed a big glass of milk and two muffins on the table in 'his' spot. "Where have you been this week? Work keeping you busy?"

He might as well come right out with it. "No, I took a week's vacation."

"In April? I thought you were saving for a trip somewhere special."

"I met a woman, Momma." He took her hand. "She's special, and she's going back to the States in a week, and—"

She stood, pulled her hand away, and stared at him like he had ten eyes. "Don't even speak to me about meeting someone from the States. You know what they do to us Puerto Ricans—love them and leave them."

"But Joy's not like th—"

"Joy? Don't say that name again in my house, you hear?"

He stood. "I'm sorry, Momma. I thought you'd be happy

for me. You would be if you'd meet her and give her a chance."

"I'm sorry, too, son. I can't do that because I want you to be happy."

He touched her shoulder, then walked to the door. "Now that I'm grown up, don't I get to choose my own happiness?"

The question repeated in his mind all the way to Ramona's—the only one he knew who might talk some sense into his mother's head.

Sadness mixed with anger at his mother for not listening to reason. How could he make her understand?

Chapter 9

WHEN Benigno arrived at the inn, Marcos told him Ramona wasn't home, and Joy hadn't returned yet either.

Benigno wrote Joy a note asking her to call him about tonight then left. What was going on with the women in his life?

How should he spend the rest of his day off? A note in the church bulletin about a work day on Saturday popped into his mind. He hadn't paid much attention, thinking he'd be working, but he would head over to the church to see if they needed some help.

Lots of cars in the parking lot. He parked and went in search of the minister.

"Benigno, *qué pasa* ?"

He turned and clasped hands with the young minister. "I've got an unexpected day off, so came to help. Is there somewhere we could work and talk in private at the same time?"

Pastor Dan stroked his goatee. "The trash cans need to be emptied and hosed out. Are you up for a stinky job?"

"Sure. It can't smell worse than I feel."

"That bad, huh?" They walked through the kitchen where Dan grabbed a box of rubber gloves. "Come on out back. I doubt anyone else will show up for this job."

They bagged the trash, sprayed and hosed out the cans, then turned them over to dry.

Dan leaned against the building. "So what's up?"

Benigno poured out the good part first—meeting Joy and thinking she might be the one. Then he told Dan his mom's reaction to the news. "I'm between a rock and a hard place like you said David was in your sermon last week."

"And what did David do?"

"Cried out to God."

"Have you done that yet?"

Benigno considered. He'd been furious at his mom and the whole situation, but he hadn't prayed about it all day. He hung his head. "Not today. I've been too angry to pray."

"David prayed when he was angry, too. Now go someplace and get on your face before God like David did, and later you can let me know what happens. I'll pray, too, and hope to meet this lovely lady soon."

Benigno drove to a park outside town and followed the pastor's advice.

LEAVING the travel agency, Joy went to find something to eat, then searched for a quiet place to call her dad.

Settling on a park bench, she prayed for wisdom and a great connection.

"Dad, it's Joy." She told him her dilemma. He listened, then gave her some surprising news of his own. "You have Asperger's? Yes, I know what it is, but how did you find out?" She listened to his tale of discovery. "I guess I need to come home soon then?" Surprised by his answer, she asked for his counselor's phone number to call on Monday. Now she would have to wait longer to talk to Ramona and Ben about her plans.

The bells of a church bonged two times. Time for her to take a bus back to the inn to rest before her big night in Old San Juan with Benigno. Her mind stuttered when she realized she'd thought his Puerto Rican name.

She said it aloud. "Benigno." It finally rolled off her tongue like words did from his mouth. Was she ready to live in Puerto Rico?

Engrossed in the sights and sounds coming through the bus windows, Joy almost missed her stop near the inn. She got off, then walked into the lobby.

Ramona's cheery smile welcomed her. "*Hola*."

"*Hola*."

"I hear you and Benigno have a big night ahead."

"*Sí*, I need to rest and get ready for it, but first I need something to drink. Can I get you anything from the kitchen?"

"No thanks, but help yourself."

Joy returned with a tall glass of lemonade.

Ramona held up her hand while talking on the phone. Finishing her call, she handed Joy a piece of paper. "Marcos said Benigno stopped by earlier. Here's the note."

"Thanks." Joy took the paper and continued down the corridor to her room. She opened the note which said "call me" with a phone number. She punched it into her phone, but it went to voice mail. "Ben, it's Joy. I just got your message. I'll be in the shower soon, but if we don't connect before five, I'll see you then."

BENIGNO arose from the mossy area where he'd knelt in prayer, not sure how long he'd prayed. Peace filled him. He walked to his car and checked his phone. His heart raced at a message from Joy. After hearing her voice, he thrilled that she sounded fine. He called back and played phone tag with her by leaving her a message. "Joy, glad to hear your voice. Try to get some rest, and I'll see you at five. Wear the dressiest clothes you brought, not that it matters. You look great in anything."

Now, to get ready, too. He hoped tonight would be a big night—for both of them.

A couple hours later he hopped in his car, dressed in navy slacks, a light blue shirt and a red, white, and blue tie.

He entered the inn and hugged Ramona who whispered in his ear, "Just wait till you see our girl."

The phrase touched him. "Our girl." If only he could say it with the bold assurance Ramona did.

He stood as he saw Joy coming down the hallway. Half

her hair was pulled up atop her head with little copper spirals coming down. It gave her the impression of being taller. Earrings like chandeliers reached to her shoulders. Her sleeveless dress of dark blue in a shimmery material hit her mid-calf with a slit up to her knees on both sides. Very fashionable, yet modest.

Speechless, Ben waited, enthralled by her loveliness. He couldn't believe she would go out with him. He'd have to fight the other guys off all night.

"Hello, Ben. Are you ready to go?"

"Yes, and uh…you look gorgeous."

She laughed as she glanced at her friend. "Ramona helped me do my hair."

Benigno winked his appreciation to *Tia* Ro then offered Joy his elbow. She took it, and they glided out the front door like walking in a dream.

As he held the door for her, he noticed several onlookers already stopping as if Joy and he were on the red carpet or something.

He rushed around to the other side, wanting to get away before something went wrong, or he awoke from this dream.

"I need to warn you that our dinner reservations are for eight, in time for the jazz music at *Carli Cafe Concierto*."

"We stopped there on our Flavors of San Juan Walking tour for a few minutes. I love jazz, and I love the idea of a concert and a meal at the same time. "

"I hoped you would."

The traffic flowed more slowly on Saturday night, but they had plenty of time to do the things he'd planned. And he would have even more time with Joy if he could convince her to stay, also part of his plan. "First, I thought we'd do the promenade down the *Paseo de la Princesa*. Have you seen it yet?"

"No, but it's on my must-see list, so that sounds great."

He continued driving until they came to the parking area by *El Capitolio* where he finally found a parking spot. As he opened her door, he said, "Now we'll ride the trolley down the coastline."

"I've been wanting to do that, too. You've planned the best night possible."

"I'm glad. I want to look at it through your gorgeous green eyes."

JOY thanked God for this man beside her. Ben was so thoughtful and flattering, nothing like her ex. She'd decided last night in bed not to think or say his name again, because he no longer had a hold on her life.

Ben assisted her in boarding the trolley. "Sit on the left where you can see the boats and water." He ushered her to a window seat before sliding in beside her.

She stared out the window, glad for this close up view of the cruise ships. Maybe she would take a cruise for her next trip. They had some great deals right now. Joy pointed. "Look at all the cruise ships in port. Is that the Atlantic Ocean?"

"We call this part of it the *Bahia de San Juan* —San

Juan Bay."

"It's stunning—so clear, and so many shades of blue and green blended together."

"*Sí*. I've often thought blue and green must be God's favorite colors."

"They're mine, too. Maybe that's why I love the ocean so much."

"I thought it must be pink since you wear that color a lot."

Joy's cheeks warmed. "My mother always told me I looked pretty in pink and bought me lots of pink clothes." She shrugged. "I guess I continue to buy clothes in that color as a way to keep her memory alive."

"I agree with your mother, pink looks wonderful on you." He stared into Joy's eyes. "I know from maps of the States that Chicago is not close to an ocean."

"You're so right. We do have beaches around the shores of Lake Michigan, but it's not the same as the ocean."

"So why do you stay there?"

"It's where my job is and my Dad, I guess."

"You need to ask yourself if you're happy there or if you would be happier elsewhere. I can't imagine living anywhere else but Puerto Rico because I am happy here, but life is too short to live someplace that doesn't make you happy."

Tears stung Joy's eyelids. "I'll think about it and pray about it."

Ben stood. "Good. We get off at the next stop. Ahead is the *Paseo de la Princesa* ." He gestured with his hand.

Turning, Joy sucked in a breath at the lovely sight before her. Past an old stone wall and two red columns, the promenade stretched as far as she could see, lined by rows of green trees on each side of the shaded walkway.

Peace stole over her heart as she strolled down the brick pathway. Various art sculptures called to her from the gardens on each side.

Ben stopped at a stately gray building. "Here is *La Princesa* which used to house prisoners, but now is home to many local art exhibits. We have time for a short visit if you'd like."

Entering, Joy's eyes widened as she drank in light, and colors, and shapes, and patterns. She turned in a full circle. "Oh, my. I don't know where to look first."

"*Sí*. This is a little hidden treasure I seek out when I need refreshment."

Joy could only nod in agreement as she made her way up and down the walls of the photo gallery. She could have spent the rest of the night here. "Thank you for introducing me to this unique place. I will have to come back again when I need to take in some more refreshment. And bring my camera."

They exited out to the street and passed a cart labeled 'Piragua.' Ben's eyes lit up. "I don't think it would spoil our late meal."

"Sounds good."

He grinned. "What kind would you like?"

"A cherry and coconut mixture, of course." She winked.

Ben's eyes twinkled. "Want to share one with two

spoons?"

"Ciertamente ."

They sat on a bench and ate the snow cone in tandem, then strolled down the promenade hand in hand.

Just when Joy thought her surprises were over, they came to the end of the walk, and the water again appeared in all its shimmering brilliance.

In front of the water towered a bronze fountain with statues of many nationalities.

"This is the *Raices* or Roots Fountain. These statues represent the many cultural heritages that make up the Puerto Rican people."

Joy noted the shadows playing on the metal, so she'd have an idea where to stand when she came back. When she glanced around, Ben sat watching her. "I need my camera here, too, so I'm ready to walk some more."

They strolled up and down the streets. She trusted Ben to get them where they needed to be at the right time, as they'd made so many turns and twists. They soon came out where they had entered the *Paseo de la Princesa*.

Her hand still in his, she followed him over a couple more streets to San Justo.

Ben glanced at his watch. "A quarter to eight. Just right." He touched the small of her back and motioned her to precede him into the building in front of them.

"Reservation, sir?"

"*Sí*, party of two at eight for Cook, *por favor* ."

"Let me make sure your table on the outdoor patio is ready."

After a couple minutes, the host returned. "Follow me, *por favor* .

As they left the room filled with white tablecloths and shining silver, Joy recalled the movies she'd seen where couples dined in places like this, such a romantic setting. She sat down at a patio table for two also decked out in linen and silver, and looked around. Even more romantic. The sky still radiated the afterglow of the sunset, while a few stars twinkled in the upper sky. A perfect place with a perfect guy.

BENIGNO drank in the sight of his lovely date in her blue-black dress with the earrings that sparkled like the stars in the blue-black sky. He wished he had a camera now.

"A penny for your thoughts." Joy grinned.

"Just thinking how blessed I am to be here with you in that gorgeous dress that matches the sky."

She looked down. "It's called midnight blue, and it's not midnight yet, but I can see what you mean. I was thinking how blessed I am to be here in such an exquisite place with such great company. I will certainly recommend this place to the next client I book for Puerto Rico."

A good opening for what I want to discuss.

A waiter stopped by and handed them each a leather-bound menu. "I shall return shortly to take your orders. What would you prefer to drink?" He looked at Joy.

"Water for me, *por favor*."

Benigno nodded. "The same." As the waiter left, he raised his menu. "I guess we should go on and see what we want. I've only eaten here once, and had the filet of salmon with mustard-cream sauce which was excellent. I've also heard the seared loin of lamb is a favorite, but feel free to choose whatever suits you."

She perused her menu, then closed it. "I think I'll try the lamb."

Their waiter appeared, and she repeated her selection to him. "Excellent choice, *señorita*."

Benigno ordered the salmon.

Soft piano music filtered into the night air from the inside performance—quiet enough where they could talk.

He swallowed and forced himself to breathe. "When you mentioned recommending people come to Puerto Rico, does that mean you plan to go back to your travel agency job?

Joy almost choked, so took a sip of water. "Yes, I do plan to continue my job as a travel agent. I enjoy what I do."

Ben frowned. "But would you consider doing the same job someplace else?"

"I've been praying about that."

His heart skipped a beat. "Really?"

"Yes, but I haven't decided yet. A lot depends on my dad."

"I see. But you are willing to consider it?"

"*Ciertamente!*"

He smiled. "Guess I'll have to live with that for now."

"Me too. Imagine how you'd feel if your mom was dead

set against you doing something."

He didn't have to imagine, he knew all about that. He would not push her anymore. At least not now. Tonight would be about just the two of them.

JOY relaxed into her chair and let the soft music calm her racing heart. She'd tried to answer Ben truthfully without getting his hopes up. She wouldn't decide anything until she spoke to her dad's counselor on Monday. It would be hard to pull off in just four days, and especially long distance, but if God was leading her to this change, she would trust Him to work it all out.

The food arrived. She took two bites. "This is heavenly. I've never had lamb so tender, and I love the vegetables, except I can't figure out what spices they're cooked in."

Ben winked. "You can always ask Ramona. She knows all the spices."

"That's true." Joy ate some more, then set down her fork and hummed along with the song the pianist played—"Love is a Many Splendored Thing." *That's also true.*

Although she'd made a self-promise not to fall in love for a long time, she wouldn't take lightly her gifts from God in leading her to Ramona and the Inn of the Dove and all the other people she'd met here, especially Ben. Time and her heart would tell if this relationship would work. She would not run ahead of God's leading again.

The pianist played another song she didn't know but still admired. People could learn new things and new places, even a new language if they wanted to. This trip had taught her that.

"Music lets us slip away into our heads, no?" Ben's low voice broke her reverie.

"*Sí*, it's so soothing, yet stirring. Sorry I got so caught up in it. You know a lot about me, so I want to learn more about you. What are your dreams and plans?"

"Although I always want Puerto Rico to be my home, I do desire to travel to many places. Do you know a good travel agent?" He quirked an eyebrow.

"A few." She smiled. "How about your plans? What would you choose if you could do anything you wanted?"

His forehead scrunched up. "I've never told anyone this, but my secret dream is to write travel articles and books. I love to read about other countries and watch TV shows about them. I know I could write one about Puerto Rico, and if that goes well, I could write about some of the other places I visit."

She slid her hand across the table to cover his. "That's an amazing dream, and you would be *so* good at it. What's holding you back?"

"I don't enjoy traveling alone. The one time Marcos and I went to Texas, the *only* state I've ever visited, we had a great time, but I know I wouldn't have enjoyed it as much without him along."

"What did you see in Texas?"

"Ranches, and cows, and horses, and more cows, and the Alamo."

"And more cows?" She laughed.

"Yes. And we learned about the history of the state and its Spanish connections."

"Learning the history of a place is my second favorite thing about traveling."

"And what is your first, Miss Travel Agent?"

"The people, of course."

Their waiter came by. "Are we ready for dessert?"

Joy glanced at her plate, surprised she'd eaten it all. She'd enjoyed the conversation and company so much she hadn't noticed.

Ben nodded. "I had the *Creme Bruleé* last time I was here, and do recommend it."

"Would you consider sharing a couple bites with me?"

"Of course." He turned to the waiter. "One *Creme Bruleé* and two forks, please."

They shared the dessert while listening to the jazz pianist play his soulful tunes. Music she could get lost in, the way she could lose herself in Benigno's blue eyes.

Chapter 10

BEN lay in bed replaying their conversation. After he opened up to her about his dream of writing travel books, she revealed even more about her love for travel—a love they shared.

They'd reached the inn and strolled past it, then had to double back. He wanted to top the night off with a real kiss, but wondered if she'd think he was trying to influence her to stay. He didn't want to use her for his own purposes like her ex had. So he settled for a kiss on the cheek in the hotel lobby before going to his car.

He'd promised to pick her up for church at nine forty-five. A glance at the clock told him he needed to be there in less than seven hours, so he'd better get some shut-eye.

When the alarm buzzed at eight, he jumped out of bed without hitting the snooze button. Less than two hours until he would see Joy again. Even that seemed too long.

Arriving at the inn before nine thirty, he shared a cup of coffee with Ramona while waiting for Joy.

Ramona smiled. "Joy told me last night was like a dream

come true for her."

"I'm glad." *I hope my dreams will soon come true.*

Joy walked down the hall in an aqua sundress skirted with ruffles in the same color.

Benigno stood. "Good morning, Joy, you remind me of one of my favorite things—ocean waves skimming the shore."

"Thanks. No one's ever told me that."

"Do you want to grab something to eat or drink before we leave?"

"I've already eaten."

He offered his elbow, and she slipped her arm inside.

After they were on their way, he turned the car stereo up a notch to one of Carli Muñoz's jazz CDs.

She closed her eyes. "Is that the same guy we listened to last evening?"

"You've got a great eye for art and a great ear for music. Yes, it's by Carli Muñoz. He's one of my favorites."

"I can see why. He's one of my new faves. I wish I'd thought to buy one of the CDs."

"We could go shopping this afternoon."

"I'd like that."

"What else would you like to do on your last Sunday here?"

She frowned. "I haven't had much time to lie on the beach, so plan to do that."

"Want some company?"

"I'd love *your* company."

"It's a date. How about a picnic on the beach?"

"Sounds fun. I like the beach so much I don't even mind a little sand in my sandwich."

He laughed, then pulled into a parking spot at Ramona's Community Church. An older building rather than the modern one he attended, but he could worship God anywhere.

JOY stared at the outside of the stately stone church. She sensed God's presence in the shh-shh of the waving palm trees surrounding it. "This is lovely. I wish I had my camera."

"I'll bring you back later today if you want to snap some photos."

"Gracias."

When she entered the sanctuary she silently prayed, "*Gracias a Dios*." Her high school French teacher had told them a foreign language was becoming part of you if you thought or prayed in that language without translating it first. Would she be able to master Spanish if her plans worked out?

Ben led her down the aisle to a bench on the left. He whispered, "This is the section where Ramona and her family usually sit. In fact, my cousin Victor Sanchez is one row up, so let's sit by him, and I'll introduce you.

He guided her to the next bench, then sat down and

leaned across Joy to speak to the man. "Hey, cuz. What brings you to San Juan today?"

"I wanted to meet Marcos' bride since I was working and couldn't make it in for their wedding."

"So you'll be at the inn after church?"

"You think I'd miss *Tia* Ramona's Sunday brunch?"

"Of course not." He looked at Joy. "Joy, I want you to meet my cousin Victor."

"Victor, this is Joy Worth from Chicago."

Joy smiled and shook Victor's hand. The music began, and everyone rose and sang, "The Lord is in His holy temple. Let all the earth keep silence before Him. Keep silence, keep silence. Keep silence before Him."

She worshipped Him in the stillness of the old church, and sensed His Spirit's presence inside her again.

After the service ended, His peace and serenity remained in her heart.

Ramona waited for them at the back. "Did you see Victor?"

Ben nodded. "Yes, and he's coming by the inn for brunch."

"Of course. He has a standing invitation just as you do. So I will see you both there? Especially since it will be Joy's last Sunday here." Ramona smiled at Joy. Was that a tear in her eye?

I wish I could tell them for sure, but don't want to raise false hopes. "Wouldn't miss it for anything."

With a hand on her back, Ben guided her to the car. "We better hurry before my cousin gets there. He's a bachelor and doesn't get to eat much home-cooking. I thought we could have a supper picnic later if that's okay with you."

"Sure." As long as it was with Ben, she didn't care what time it happened.

AS soon as they'd eaten, Benigno stood. "Hate to leave good company and great food, but I promised Joy we'd go shop for some Carli Muñoz CDs, then come back for R and R on the beach."

Joy rose. "I need to run back to the room and grab my camera."

After she left, Victor raised his eyebrows at Benigno. "Does that R and R include sunbathing?"

"It might, and a picnic supper, and a moonlight stroll on the beach."

"Too bad I have to head back to Fajardo soon."

Ben gave a fake grin. "Yeah, too bad."

Marcos and Teresa laughed.

Joy joined them, and gave a quizzical look. "Did I miss anything?"

"No, but I've missed you."

Victor made a groan.

Benigno escorted Joy to the car. Sharing was over-rated. He needed her all to himself.

Joy found two CDs she wanted, and he insisted on buying them as his gift to her since he'd introduced her to

Muñoz. He also helped her find some small gifts for her co-workers. "Ready to head to the beach?"

"You never have to ask me twice to go to the beach."

They stopped by the church so Joy could take a few pictures of the inside and outside of the building, then drove to the inn.

Ben carried his backpack. I'm going to change in *Tia* Ro's apartment. Meet you out on the beach in ten?"

"Sounds like a plan."

He was sitting in a lounge chair when Joy approached wearing a pink and navy one piece suit with a halter top and a navy sarong. Very becoming.

She laid her things on the table next to him. "Is this place taken?"

"It's promised to the prettiest gal on the beach." He winked.

"So I don't need to move?"

"You better not, or I'll have to chase you down."

She giggled and cocked an eyebrow. "I'll keep that in mind." She sat down and sprayed lots of sunscreen over her legs, arms, and chest. Then she spread her chair and towel out flat and lay on her back. "Don't let me sleep long."

That would be easy. No way he could sleep with her so close. "Sure. How long?"

"Thirty minutes, I guess, then I'll roll over."

He checked his watch, and set an alarm just in case. When it buzzed he was relieved he had, as the warmth from the sand and the sun had knocked him out. Or maybe it was

Tia Ro's carb-laden buffet.

"Time to turn, my dear." Had he spoken those words aloud?

She asked him to spray sunscreen on her back then lay on her stomach. "Thirty more minutes, then let's go for a walk."

"Okay." He set the watch alarm again.

He forced himself to stay awake. Unless he could convince her to stay, he only had four more days with her, and didn't want to waste any of it snoozing.

JOY sat up when the alarm went off. "I'm ready to stretch my legs."

"We do need to work up an appetite before supper." He stood and helped her to her feet.

"I agree." She applied more sunscreen then wrapped the sarong around her waist.

As they strolled down the beach, he reached for her hand.

It seemed the most natural thing in her world to be walking hand in hand with Ben on a sunny beach in Puerto Rico. Something she hoped would become part of her day more often if...

She would know tomorrow if her plan would work. Joy prayed it would.

After several minutes of walking, she nodded toward their spot on the beach. "I'm ready to go read awhile. How about you?"

"I didn't bring a book today, so thought I'd get in and body surf."

Before Ben left, he offered her a Coco Rico.

"Thanks."

She watched as his trim body entered the water, then as he surfaced and shook off the droplets. Like a movie star.

He soon returned and lay on the chair beside hers.

After another hour, she stood. "I think I've had enough sun for today. I'm going to shower this sand off. What time do you want to meet for our picnic and stroll?"

"Seven on the back veranda?"

"See you then."

After showering, Joy phoned her dad again to make sure he had spoken to his counselor about her phone call the next day. Her father talked more than she ever remembered, which made her wonder if this diagnosis and plan could be the best for him.

She lay down across her bed, not physically tired, but emotionally drained. So much had happened this past couple weeks, and if her plan worked, many more changes would occur soon. *Life is about change, Lord, and if You are in these changes, then I trust everything will work out.*

At six-thirty she dressed in a long, white sundress. She applied a little mascara, and pulled her hair back into a band, then changed her mind, and let it down. Her cheeks glowed pink from the sun.

Ready or not, here I come, Benigno.

BENIGNO waited on the veranda. He stood as she approached with the setting sun at her back bronzing the copper glints in her curls. His heart beat in his ears. He wanted so much to tell her how he loved her, but had to hold it in until she was ready to hear it.

"Last night you were beautiful. Tonight you are gorgeous! I won't be able to take my eyes off you to eat."

She shook her head. "Silly man. Of course you can, even if I have to feed you myself."

His eyebrows arched. "That's the best idea I've heard all day."

"Have you been planning this ever since I fed you breakfast on the way to Icacos?"

"No, but now that you mention it, it's a very appealing idea." He lifted the large picnic basket. "Ready to go?"

She joined her arm with his.

Pink, purple, mauve, and golden streaks fanned out across the horizon as they approached the beach. Even the sky couldn't compare to her beauty.

Opening the basket, he pulled out a crisp, white tablecloth, then set out real china and silverware. Next he placed several covered bowls and serving spoons. He lifted two seat cushions from some beach chairs and placed them next to each other on the sand, then pulled out a towel and draped it across his arm. "Dinner is served, *señorita*."

She dropped to a cushion and tucked her skirt around her

legs.

Benigno sat beside her and opened two bowls. "For our soup we have *Asopao*."

"My favorite."

Next he uncovered seared loin of lamb with vegetables.

"Another favorite."

"We aim to please."

She glanced at another bowl, still covered. "What's for dessert?"

"You'll have to eat your supper to find out. Let's thank God for our food." He reached for her hand that fit his like God had made them from the same cloth. "Father, I thank You for this food and for this special person to share it with. Bless us and use us for Your purposes and to Your praise. In Your Son's name, Amen."

Joy lifted her head, and he spied tears in her eyes. Happy tears, he hoped.

They ate while watching the sky fade to purple and indigo. The first star popped out as he reached for the dessert. "Close your eyes. You have to guess what it is from the aroma."

She complied, and he held it under her nose. "Ummm. *Creme Bruleé*."

He laughed. "You're a hard woman to surprise."

"This whole vacation has been God's surprise for me. And you're a big part of His blessings."

His gaze locked with hers. "I'm glad."

Leaning over, his lips touched hers as his arm encircled

her waist and pulled her closer.

She returned his kiss. Could this night get any better?

JOY lay in her bed reliving Ben's kiss and their moonlight stroll. She'd never kissed anyone with that much passion. Ben certainly knew how to kiss, although he'd assured her he'd rarely dated or kissed anyone. Was it chemistry between them or what? Could it be love?

She went to sleep pondering the question, and awoke with it still on her mind. Was love the reason she wanted to remain in Puerto Rico? She hoped she'd get to stay long enough to find out.

Jumping out of bed, she needed to hurry and eat, then call her dad's counselor at ten, which would be nine Chicago time. Everything depended on that phone call. Now that her dad was doing much better, she couldn't bear the idea of letting him down, making him relapse back into his former non-communicative self.

Marcos met her at the desk. "Good morning, *Señorita* Joy. What are your travel plans today?"

"I'm not sure. I think Ben has something planned for this afternoon, but I need to do several personal things this morning."

"Have a good day."

"You too." What would she do if this day turned into a bad day, or even a horrible day? *God, please calm my fears. I will trust in You.*

She drank some juice, then stuffed an apple in her pocket in case she got hungry before Ben picked her up at one. She walked to a local park she'd discovered. Not crowded at nine o'clock. Hopefully, it would be even more deserted by ten. She walked and prayed, then sat and prayed, then walked some more. At ten AM she sat and glanced around. Only one other person in sight. She dialed the number Dad had given her.

"Good morning. Barbara Perkins' office."

"Hello. My name is Joy Worth, and I believe Ms. Perkins is expecting my call."

"Yes, Miss Worth. I will connect you now."

Two buzzes crossed the line before a soft voice said, "Hello, Miss Worth. I am so glad to hear from you. Your dad wants me to explain what he's been through with his Asperger's. He'd never been diagnosed before he came to me a few weeks ago, although he told me your mother had mentioned the possibility before she died. After her death, he withdrew further into himself, so never pursued it until his boss asked him to try counseling. Since he'd heard the word before from your mom, he was willing to listen to me, and to try to learn to handle it more effectively. Do you have any questions?"

"Do you think dad can get along on his own right now?"

"That's our goal, and he's making great strides. In fact, that's why he and I agree it would be helpful for you to wait a few weeks before returning to Chicago. He's just starting to get out and do tasks on his own. If you moved back in right now, he might have a tendency to let you take over his daily needs again. I'd like him to be more settled in handling things himself first. Do you understand?"

"Yes, that part makes sense. I noticed as a child how he wanted my mother to handle everything except his work, and when I moved back in with him, the same pattern repeated itself."

"Your dad is very capable at work where he feels comfortable with computers and minimal interaction with others. His boss wanted to give him a promotion and more responsibilities, and that's when the company sent him to me to figure out why he was rejecting the new job."

"I see. So how long do you think I should stay away?"

"A month or more, longer would probably be better. Is that going to be a problem?"

"Not at all. I've already lined up a part time temporary job at the travel agency my agency worked with in Puerto Rico. I can't afford to stay at the inn long-term, so will need to find other lodging, but I'm learning my way around San Juan pretty well, so that shouldn't be a problem."

"You sound like a very resourceful young woman. I see why your dad is so proud of you. He said he's amazed how well you turned out without much help from him."

"He always met all my physical needs, so he was a good dad in many ways. We just never related emotionally. I hope that will change in the future."

"I understand. I know this is a lot to process. Feel free to call me later with any more questions, and touch base by the end of the month to see what kind of progress he's making. He wants to share his growth with you. He even mentioned coming to visit you in Puerto Rico."

"He told me, and I would love that. You think it's a possibility?"

"Yes, I think that's a great goal for him."

"Okay, I appreciate your time, Ms. Perkins, and will call back by the end of April if not before. Thank you."

"Thank you. Your father is fortunate to have such a caring daughter."

Joy sat with the phone in her hand until someone jogging by startled her. She wanted to talk to her dad, but knew he didn't like calls at work, so decided to walk around more before going back to the inn. Arriving at the local travel agency, she told the manager she could start the following Monday, and they worked out a few details.

As her phone buzzed again, she was surprised when her dad's number appeared. "Dad. How are you?"

"I'm fine. Ms. Perkins told me you all agreed it would be best for you to stay there at least a month."

"Yes, I'll miss you, but we can stay in touch by phone."

"I miss you, too. And I want to come to see you as soon as I can work out all the details. Ms. Perkins thinks I need to make all the plans myself."

"That would be great, Dad. I know you can do it."

"Well, I'm at work, so I better go."

"Okay. Love you."

"Love you, too."

Her dad said he loved her—for the first time she could remember. This was a day she'd never forget.

BENIGNO arrived at the inn a few minutes early, not wanting to waste any of their precious time left together. He checked at the desk, and when Ramona told him Joy was still out, he said he would wait for her on the front porch.

As she entered the gate, her smile struck him, even before she saw him. She must've had a good morning.

He arose from the chair. "Joy?"

She looked at him, then threw her arms around him in a hug.

"I'll meet you here every day if I get that kind of reception."

"You're crazy."

"Crazy about you."

She laughed. "I've got some news for you. And Ramona. Is she here?"

"She's in the lobby."

Joy grabbed his hand. "Let's go, and I'll tell you both my good news."

She'd said 'good news.' He hoped he would think so, too.

"Ramona, can you come and sit with us a few minutes?" Joy's eyes danced.

"*Ciertamente*. You must have had a great morning."

"I did, and I want to tell you and Ben at the same time."

They sat in the lobby chairs. He looked at Joy, who fidgeted like a kid at Christmas.

"I talked to my dad and his counselor this morning. He

has Asperger's."

Ramona's forehead scrunched. "Is that a form of autism?"

"It's high-functioning autism. He understands well, but can't always communicate with people. His boss wanted to promote him, but Dad had trouble accepting the changes, so the boss sent him to a counselor who diagnosed him."

"That's good, isn't it?" Ben still wasn't sure.

"Yes, and the counselor has set up a plan for him to do more on his own, so…" She looked from him to Ramona "…she thinks I should stay here at least another month."

"That's definitely good news, great news!" Ben's head spun.

"I think so, too." Ramona smiled. "Do you need a place to stay?"

"Yes, I was going to ask if you knew anyone who might rent by the month. I'm going to work at the local travel agency part-time, but can't afford to stay here at daily rates."

"How about you help me at the desk and maybe take some pictures and make me a new brochure? I think we can work out a swap for room and board."

"Really? That would be wonderful if I can stay here."

Ramona stood and held out her hand, and Joy shook it. "It's a deal then. Now I'll let you two talk."

Ben rose and cupped Joy's elbow. "Let's go to the back veranda."

JOY followed him to their familiar meeting spot. She could get used to his leading her, especially if she could stay longer than a month. Hope rose in her heart.

Ben's eyes locked on hers. Her gaze locked on his. Did she read love there?

She broke the silence. "You know I may have to move back in a month, maybe even travel to the States often to check on my dad."

"That would be okay. God is in our relationship, so I trust Him to work all the kinks out. I'm just thankful we'll have more time for me to show you how much I love you."

She gasped.

"I do love you, Joy and have wanted to tell you for days, but was afraid it was too soon. Now, I have another whole month to tell you and show you and—"

Joy stopped his words with a kiss—a long, heartfelt, tingle-to-her-toes kiss. A never-let-go kiss. "I love you, too, Benigno."

His eyes gleamed. "You called me Benigno."

"I did, because it's your name, and I love you and your name."

"Let's seal it with another kiss."

"You'll get no argument from me."

Chapter 11

AS he entered the Inn of the Dove, Benigno glanced around. This second-home had become even more familiar to him the past few weeks. Joy had been in Puerto Rico almost two months now. She planned to return to Chicago to check on her dad next week and talk to him about later visiting her in Puerto Rico.

Benigno's mother had softened and allowed him to bring Joy by the house. They had hit it off like he knew they would.

He loved Joy, and she loved him, so he wanted to propose to her before she left. Only one thing stopped him from popping the question—would it be too soon for her? Two months ago, she'd been engaged to someone else, and she'd told him sometimes she still doubted her decision-making ability. He'd prayed and prayed for God to show him the best moment. How long would he have to wait?

"Hi Marcos."

"Hi, cuz. Joy just ran back to her room to grab her cell phone."

"Thanks. I told her it would be easier to hold onto while zipping through the rain forest." Benigno turned toward Joy as she approached. "*Hola*. Ready to go ziplining today?"

"How did he convince you to try it?" Marcos' eyes gleamed.

Joy grinned. "I've added several new activities to my repertoire since I came here. Time to check another one off my Puerto Rico bucket list."

Benigno chuckled, and his heart warmed at the freedom in Joy's voice. She had come so far, but was she ready to go even further? "The beautiful weather is awaiting us at *El Yunque*, so *vámonos*."

She linked her arms in his, a gesture full of trust that always made his heart switch into a faster gear. "Lead on."

He wanted their lives linked like this, if she were ready. *God, show me the right time.*

The drive to the rain forest flew by with happy conversation punctuated by short bits of comfortable silence.

Joy shifted toward him. "Will you be leading this tour today?"

"Yes, but you'll be getting the deluxe personal tour—just you and me."

The golden flecks in her eyes shone. "Thanks. That's special."

And you are so special to me.

WHEN they arrived, Joy hopped out and scanned the

lush, tropical greenery. Her eyes roamed from the tops of one treetop to the next. In minutes, she'd be whizzing between them. Fear and excitement gripped her stomach. Another adventure. Her world and heart had been turned upside down and inside out on this trip. She'd learned about love and how to take on new, sometimes frightening things. How much she'd have missed if she hadn't come—especially this man walking beside her.

As they approached the first tower, several workers waved at Benigno.

One man winked at him, then elbowed him in the ribs. "We're glad to meet the beautiful Joy you have been spending so much time with."

Benigno laughed. "Just remember she's my gal, guys."

My gal. The words thrilled Joy, and she couldn't contain her wide smile.

One of the men strapped Benigno into the safety harness. As Benigno fastened each buckle on her, her heart galloped, but she would not back down.

He stared into her eyes. "You wish me to go first?"

She nodded. They'd discussed this on the drive over.

"I'll be waiting on the next platform to catch you." He gave her a hug and whispered in her ear. "I'm so proud of you for overcoming your fears."

Joy's bright smile dimmed a bit. Ben pushed off. The line whined for the few seconds it took for him to reach the platform.

He gripped the railing, then swung around and waved to her.

The guide standing next to her raised an eyebrow. "Ready to fly?"

Unable to speak, Joy nodded. She shuddered at the metallic click and tug as he tested the harness. He pointed toward a painted square on the wooden platform. "Stand here."

Joy closed her eyes, and only had time to draw a single breath before strong hands pressed against her back and sent her flying off the edge of the platform. White knuckled, she gripped the straps connected to the harness. She heard the scritch of the clip and a strangled moan from her mouth, muffled by air brushing by her face.

When she opened her eyes, she was safe in Benigno's arms. The breath she'd held the whole way whooshed out. "I'm so glad you're here."

"Me too." He kissed her nose. "Ready for the next one?"

Her hands shook, and she tried to hold her voice steady. "As ready as I'll ever be." She tried to make it sound like a joke, but the thought of swinging through the air again still terrified her.

Benigno pulled her into a hug and whispered in her ear. "I'll be praying as you fly. Try to open your eyes this time for the video." He pushed off again. When he reached the next tower, he raised his phone.

God, help me. She stepped to the edge and forced her eyes to stay open on the flight over. A spectacular view.

Ben's arms reached out for her, and she fell into them, almost toppling them both. "Steady now. How was that?"

"Still a little daunting, but once I noticed the scenery, I

forgot to be scared."

He smiled, revealing his dimple. "That's my girl. Try to smile for the video this time."

She pulled her iPhone out of her zippered bag. "I plan to video you on your trip over this time." She shot his flight, then put the phone away before letting another worker push her off.

At the next stand, she suggested she go first so she could take Benigno from the front. As she flew over, she lifted up her praise to God for His beauty all around her.

Benigno flew to her with his arms out like a bird. The guy on the tower shouted, "Superman!"

He straightened his legs before reaching the tower. "If you decide to try to be Superwoman, be sure to let your legs drop to slow you down before you land."

"I don't think you have to worry about that."

After a few more runs, they had to walk and climb a higher tower for their next sets. When they reached the top, she scanned the perfect blue sky over the green treetops, and was so caught up in God's creation she didn't even feel the push. The sensation of flying overcame her, and her arms went out like she could hug God.

Benigno caught her in his arms as she came to a sudden stop. "Wow! You're really getting into this." He chuckled.

"I am. Can I go first next time?"

"Sure."

She couldn't wait to feel and hear the wind in her face. It was as if God were blowing his breath on her, filling her up with more of Him.

When Benigno arrived, he quirked an eyebrow at her. "Ready to go faster?"

"How can we do that?"

"If we take a tandem trip on a downhill run, our weight will make the flight faster."

She grinned. "Let's go."

The worker hooked up Benigno first, then helped her onto his back before hooking her up. They shot off the platform and into the sky.

ARRIVING at the next platform, Benigno slowly stood up straight to let her slide off his back.

When he turned, in front of him danced Joy's beautiful eyes, filled with gold flecks of sunlight. "Glad we came?"

She threw her arms around his neck and kissed him until the zipline worker cleared his throat. "Sorry. I had to show you how much I loved this."

"No apologies needed. I'm enjoying it just as much." *Or maybe more.*

Joy did a three-hundred-and-sixty degree turn. "I can see for miles."

"Yes, it's one of the highest platforms." He pointed to her right. "What do you see over there?"

Her voice quieted with awe. "Is that the ocean?"

"*Sí*, it is the Atlantic." He tucked a wisp of her silky tresses back.

"And it has even more shades of blue and green than usual."

"I agree. Only God could create such a spectacular scene." *And only God could love you more than I do.* He put an arm around her waist, and they stood for several moments admiring God's handiwork. "Do you want to go first or last on our final zip?"

"Last because I know you'll catch me."

I certainly will. Benigno winked, then sailed off toward the ground.

Landing, he whipped out his iPhone to video her last ride of the day. It wouldn't be her last ride. Not after the way she'd enjoyed the last few flights.

She came down like Superwoman again—straight into his arms—where he hoped she'd stay forever.

He pulled out a couple water bottles and handed one to her, then gulped his down. "Let's hike to the ranger center to pick up our picnic lunch."

"I am hungry after all that flying."

They started down the narrow trail, Joy in front.

At a rustling of branches Benigno attempted to look around her, but before he could move, a tall man running through the trees plowed into Joy, knocking her against a tall Ausubo tree. The man kept on running.

Dropping to the ground beside her, Benigno smoothed her hair back from her head. A bump above her right eye was the only mark he saw. "Joy, are you all right?"

No answer. Only the wind blowing through the trees.

He looked up. Dread grabbed his heart. *God help us.*

A young man jogged toward them. "Did you see a tall man running through here?"

"Yes, he knocked my girlfriend into this tree. She's unconscious."

The man dropped down onto his knees. "He stole my wife's bag with all our belongings."

"I'll phone it in." His voice shook. "I need to call for a g…gurney to carry her out."

He made the call, then prayed for the medics to hurry and for Joy to revive soon.

The seconds ticked off like hours.

Two of his medic friends arrived in less than ten minutes and carefully loaded Joy onto the gurney, then carried her out to the ambulance.

Benigno followed in his car to the nearest hospital. How could this accident happen? Joy had lived up to her name all morning, and now this? *Forgive me, Father. I will trust in You.*

He gave the lady at the desk Joy's medical information from her zipped bag. He called *Tia* Ro. He prayed and paced the emergency waiting room.

Finally a doctor appeared and announced Joy's name. Benigno approached him. "How is she, Doctor?"

"Still unconscious, I am afraid, although the CAT scan did not tell us why. Sometimes these injuries must take time. We are moving her to a regular room. Wait about five minutes then come to room 205."

Benigno nodded. He waited a couple minutes, then sped down the hall, and peeked into the room. His beautiful Joy lay lifeless like Sleeping Beauty in the old Disney movie, her hair fanned out around her, the copper highlights glinting in the sun. The bump on her forehead had doubled in size. That was a good sign, right?

"Joy, please wake up if you can hear me."

Dropping to the side of the bed, he held onto her hand, needing to connect in some way. "God, please heal this woman you brought into my life and into my heart. In Your Son's precious name. Amen."

He prayed more, then kissed her hand. "Joy, I need you to wake up and talk to me." His thumb traced the outline of her soft cheek.

No answer. Just the ticking of the clock on the wall. "I've been waiting for the right time to ask you to marry me. We've only known each other a couple months, but I'm certain you are the woman I want to marry—the woman God brought to me. I'll wait as long as it takes. We can have a long engagement if you want, but please awaken and say you will marry me."

JOY could hear, but couldn't force her eyes open. Benigno had been praying for her, and now he was asking her to marry him.

Marry him?

Singing swirled around and over her. She recognized God's voice, and was enveloped in His love. *Gracias a Dios, for bringing me to this island. And for helping me surrender to you and hear Your voice singing over me again*. She basked in his loving Presence.

After a few minutes, the singing faded, and another voice pierced her brain. Benigno.

Her eyes blinked open, and she stared into the blue eyes of the man she loved. "Yes. I will."

THE END

Translations

Adios — Good-bye

Americano — An American

Asopao — a traditional soup

Bahia de San Juan — San Juan Bay

Buenas dias — Good day (Good morning)

chica (*chicas*) — lovely young girl(s)

Ciertamente — certainly

coqui — a small tree frog with a very loud chirp

de nada — literally meaning it's nothing. Used in place of don't mention it or you're welcome

gracias — Thanks

gracias a Dios — Thanks be to God

hasta la vista — so long (good-bye)

Hola — Hi (Hello)

la cola — any cola drink

limonada — lemonade

Mamá — Mother, mom

mi amiga — my female friend

mi familia — my family

mi querida — my dear

Muchas gracias — Thanks very much

por favor — please (if you please)

qué pasa — what's up (what's going on)

Raices — Roots Fountain

restaurante (*restaurantes*) — restaurant (restaurants)

Señora — Mrs. (A married woman)

Señorita — Miss (An unmarried woman)

Sí — yes

Tia — aunt

Creme Bruleé — a fired French dessert which is to carmelize the sugar

Touché — a French term traditionally used to acknowledge that one's fencing opponent has just drawn blood, now used to admit that someone has made a clever or effective point in an argument

MAP OF PUERTO RICO

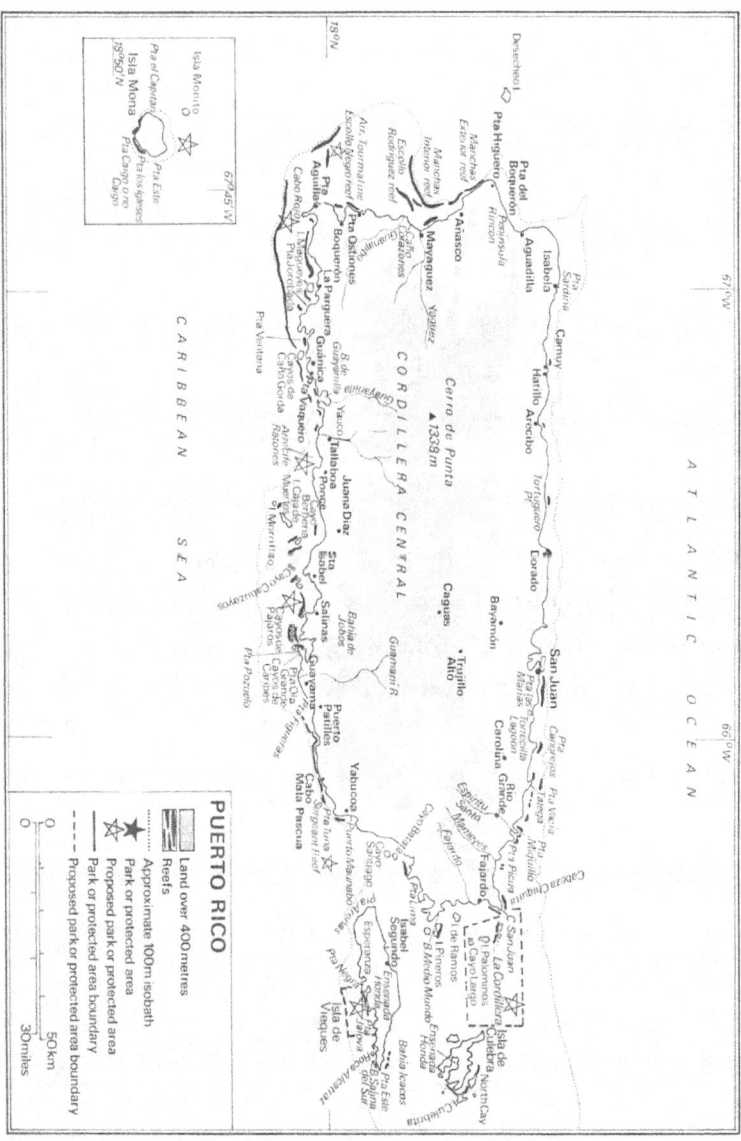

Courtesy of the U.S. Geological Survey Coral Health and Monitoring
Program: http://www.coral.noaa.gov/

Discussion Questions

I have enjoyed writing about Puerto Rico, and my husband was sweet enough to accompany me on a trip to this beautiful country so I could better describe the sights and scenery. It is truly a country blessed with much of God's beautiful creation, and I am so glad I got to journey there. Maybe this story will inspire you to want to travel there also.

Following are some suggested discussion questions I hope will uplift and encourage you in your faith walk.

Joy Worth used to hear God's voice before she stopped listening to Him because she wanted to get married so badly.

1. Have you ever done something like this or known someone who has?

2. Was the outcome as disastrous as Joy's?

This book begins with the Bible verse Zephaniah 3:17.

3. Do you believe God still sings over us with His love as it says in Zephaniah 3:17?

4. Do you think sometimes we don't realize God still sings over us because our lives are too busy to stop and listen?

5. Have you ever heard God singing over you like Joy did at the end of the book? If so, how did it feel?

At times in the story, both Joy and Benigno feel as if the situation looks hopeless. Read Ephesians 3:20 and then consider the following:

6. Has God ever taken a hopeless situation and changed it into something better than you could have asked or imagined as He did for Joy?

Mofongo Recipe

MOFONGO RECIPE

The dish called *Mofongo* referred to in this story can be made several different ways, so I will tell you a couple here, but it is open to substitutes, so feel free to use or add other ingredients you like, too.

INGREDIENTS:

4 green plantains, peeled and sliced into rounds

3 TBS plus reserve 1 TBS extra virgin olive oil

3 to 4 cloves (to taste) fresh garlic, minced

dash to pinch (to taste) salt (Kosher or sea salt is best)

1 cup: any meat you prefer

> Traditional meats range anywhere from chicken or various seafoods all the way to pork cracklings or shredded pork .

 ## SUPPLIES:

measuring cups/spoons

good sharp knife/cutting board

sauté pan

pot or basin to soak plantains

food processor or potato masher or mortar & pestle

 ## PREPARATION:

Peel and slice the plantains and soak in salted water

Mince the garlic

Prepare the meat if necessary (shred, etc.)

 ## DIRECTIONS:

Soak the plantain in salted water for 10-15 minutes. Drain and sauté the plantain slices in 3 TBS medium hot oil for 10-12 minutes until done, but not crispy.

In food processor, or with potato masher, or using a mortar & pestle (the authentic way!) mash the plantains with the garlic, salt, and 1 TBS extra virgin olive oil until smooth. Stir in the meat.

Form this mixture into balls by hand (several small or 2-4 large ones) and serve warm, or serve the balls with some rich stew ladled over the top. I even read one recipe that suggested deep frying the balls before serving, but I will leave that option to your judgment.

Acknowledgements

ALL thanks to God for putting such wonderful Christian friends in my path to work with on this book: Gregg and Hallee Bridgeman, MaryAnn Diorio, Lynette Sowell, and Vasthi Reyes Acosta.

Gregg and Hallee are both consummate professionals in the writing field and much more knowledgeable about publishing than I ever hope to be. I appreciate their help so much, but any mistakes are my own.

If MaryAnn, Vasthi, and Lynette hadn't already been to Puerto Rico, my story may never have come to fruition, and I might not have traveled there to experience such a beautiful country and people. I also appreciate Jen Johnson and Jackie Layton who helped in the brainstorming stage, along with Loretta Gibbons who also read and critiqued the whole story. Joy Liddy also critiqued part of the story.

A big thanks to Unity Christian Church Book Club ladies who always encourage me and most of all pray for my writing.

A special thanks to my wonderful husband who also read every page of this story aloud with me to help me hear the mistakes, and who traveled to the beautiful island of Puerto Rico with me and encourages me in all my writing endeavors.

May all glory be to God who called me to be His own and to write for Him. Please know that His Word says He calls us all to follow Him, so if you do not know Him, I pray you will call out to Him and find a Bible-preaching church to worship Him and fellowship with other believers.

[9] *... if you confess with your mouth the Lord Jesus and believe in your heart that God has raised Him from the dead, you will be saved.* [10] *For with the heart one believes unto righteousness, and with the mouth confession is made unto salvation. ...* [13] *For "whoever calls on the name of the Lord shall be saved."*

Romans 10:9-10,13 (NKJV)

MORE GREAT STORIES

More Great Reads

IF you enjoyed reading *Surrender to Peace*, be sure to check out even more great reads by Rose Allen McCauley.

Christmas Belles of Georgia
by Rose Allen McCauley, Jeanie Smith Cash,
Jeri Odell and Debra Ullrick

Christmas Grace
by Rose Allen McCauley

Excerpt: Christmas Grace

PLEASE enjoy this special excerpt from *Christmas Belles of Georgia*.

NICK couldn't believe Christmas Day had finally arrived. He stopped in front of the B and B and rang the now familiar bell.

Carol opened the door, a package spilling out of her arms.

Judging from the gaily-wrapped boxes, Carol had been in her element shopping for Phyllis and her girls. "Did you leave anything for the other customers?"

"A few things. Did you get the bikes?"

"Yep. They're already loaded." He started picking up boxes to carry out. "Who is that other sack of presents for?"

She winked. "One might be for you, and the rest are for my sisters."

"I thought you only had three sisters."

"I do, but they have to receive two each—one for Christmas and one for our birthday."

Thanks to Mrs. B, he had two gifts for Carol. "Speaking of birthdays, happy birthday to the sweetest girl of all. And I do have two gifts for you, too, but they're wrapped together. Do you want them now or after we deliver these presents?"

"Later. I can't wait to see the kids' expressions when they see their bikes and all the other gifts."

"Me either." *And I can't wait to watch you open yours.*

After a couple trips, the truck was loaded, and they drove the familiar blocks.

Each gathered up an armful of boxes then approached the house. As they set down the presents, they noticed a plate of decorated Christmas cookies with a note.

Carol read the note, and began to cry. Nick slid it out of her hands, hoping and praying nothing was wrong. It read:

Dear Jesus' helpers, we so much appreciate all your gifts, so wanted to share some of our Christmas cookies with you—cookies made with the flour, butter, sugar and eggs you provided. We also wanted to share our mom's favorite Bible verse about the greatest gift of all. "Thanks be to God for His indescribable gift." 2 Corinthians 9:15. Love, Phyllis, Yvonne, and Connie

Nick swiped at his own eyes, then lifted the plate of cookies and took Carol by the hand to go back for the bicycles. When they reached the truck, he whispered, "What's wrong?"

She sniffled. "Nothing. Did you read the verse?"

"Yes, it's one of my favorites, but why are you crying?"

She lifted the card she'd taped to one of the bicycles. He read it then looked at her, amazed. Carol had chosen the same verse. "A God-incidence?"

"Definitely. Only He could have so perfectly orchestrated everything."

They rolled the bikes to the edge of the porch. Carol waved Nick to go first, so he hid in the bushes while she rang the bell and ran.

She snuggled in next to him as the children oohed and aahed over the bikes and other boxes.

The math-whiz youngest daughter counted each present. "…eleven…twelve. I told you it would be twelve today. I wonder if we'll get thirteen tomorrow and—"

Phyllis shushed her. "Remember the song 'The Twelve Days of Christmas'?"

Both girls nodded.

"Today is Christmas, so there is no need for further gifts. It's Jesus' birthday so let's go sing 'Happy Birthday' to Him and decide how we can surprise someone else next year on the twelve days of Christmas. Deal?" The girls smacked palms. "Deal."

As the girls entered the house, Phyllis stepped out on the porch and looked straight at them, although he didn't know if she could see them or just sensed their presence. "Thank you, and God bless you. Merry Christmas!"

Nick's heart swelled with love for others, his Lord who had worked all this out, and for the best God-incidence in his life—the precious woman who knelt beside him. The one he wanted by his side for the rest of his life.

He pulled Carol to her feet. "Come on. We've got one more Christmas party to attend."

Excerpt: Christmas Belles of Georgia

PLEASE enjoy this special excerpt from *Christmas Grace*.

SOMEONE started up the sound system with music from a decade ago. "We Belong Together" by Mariah Carey. Chris liked the words, but hoped for a few slower tunes.

As they walked out on the dance floor, someone bumped into them. Chris couldn't remember her name, but he smelled alcohol on her breath.

The girl stared into Grace's eyes and spoke in a loud voice. "You were one of those Three Musketeers, weren't you? Or is it the Two Musketeers now?" She cackled.

All color drained from Grace's face, She ran out the door and down the hall. JoJo came over and escorted the inebriated woman out the front door.

Chris took off down the hall. Where would she have gone? He kept walking until he stopped at the sound of someone crying in the girls' bathroom. He leaned against the wall and waited. And waited. Finally, he hollered into the restroom. "Grace, are you in there?" No answer. "If you don't come out in one minute, I'm coming in."

He waited two minutes then barged in. He found her standing in front of the mirrors trying to remove the black streaks around her eyes and down her face with paper towels. He took the towels from her hand. "Let me try." He put a little soap on a towel then added a little water. He rubbed softly to no avail. Next, he tried harder pressure, until she stole the towel back.

"It's not going to work. I used waterproof mascara first, but when it ran out, I put some other mascara on top, so I'm going to look like a raccoon until I get some make-up remover."

He traced one of her streaks with his finger. "You're the prettiest raccoon I ever saw." He drew in a deep breath of her scent. "And you smell a whole lot better than one, too." Pulling her into his arms, he kissed her.

She kissed him back.

Still in his arms, Grace began to laugh until black tears streamed down her face.

Chris joined in the laughter until he cried, too. "What will our friends say if they come looking for us?"

"They'll say…snuff-snuff, you pulled a stunt to…sniff-sniff, top all the others you did in high school—kissing in the girls' restroom."

"I love you, my funny little raccoon." And he did.

Testimony

I grew up the oldest of seven kids in a very noisy, busy house. My husband and I raised three children, and are now blessed with five grandchildren, so our home is often busy and noisy also. I love it when we can all get together. But the older I get, the more I crave quiet and peace. I find it harder to concentrate with noise around, and have been practicing the stillness of quietude in the morning and evenings to help me pray and hear and discern God's voice better.

I hope you will find some time after you have read this book to practice being quiet in God's presence. Then read your Bible or the verses I mentioned above, and ask God what He wants to say to you. If you want to know more about Him, the book of John is a great place to start, especially John 3:16.

Know that as I wrote this story, I prayed for those who would read it to receive the blessing God had for them. God bless you, and feel free to contact me on my website at: www.rosemccauley.com

About the Author

Rose Allen McCauley has been writing for over ten years and her written words have reached thousands of hearts through her contributions to several non-fiction anthologies and devotionals. A retired schoolteacher, she has been happily married to her college sweetheart for over four decades. Rose is a mother to three grown children and grandmother to five lovely, lively grandkids!

Reared in the largest city in Kentucky, Rose has lived on a farm of almost four hundred acres for the past forty-two years, but is in the process of moving to a small town in Kentucky. She loves to read and write small town stories.

If you have a small town story you'd like to share, please stop by her website and leave a comment. She would love to hear from you. Also find Rose on twitter @RoseAMcCauley and Facebook at http://on.fb.me/1LrXNoS

Connect with Rose online: www.rosemccauley.com

Find Rose Online

Author site:

http://www.rosemccauley.com

Facebook:

http://on.fb.me/1LrXNoS

Twitter:

https://twitter.com/RoseAMcCauley